TOLKIEN'S BAG END

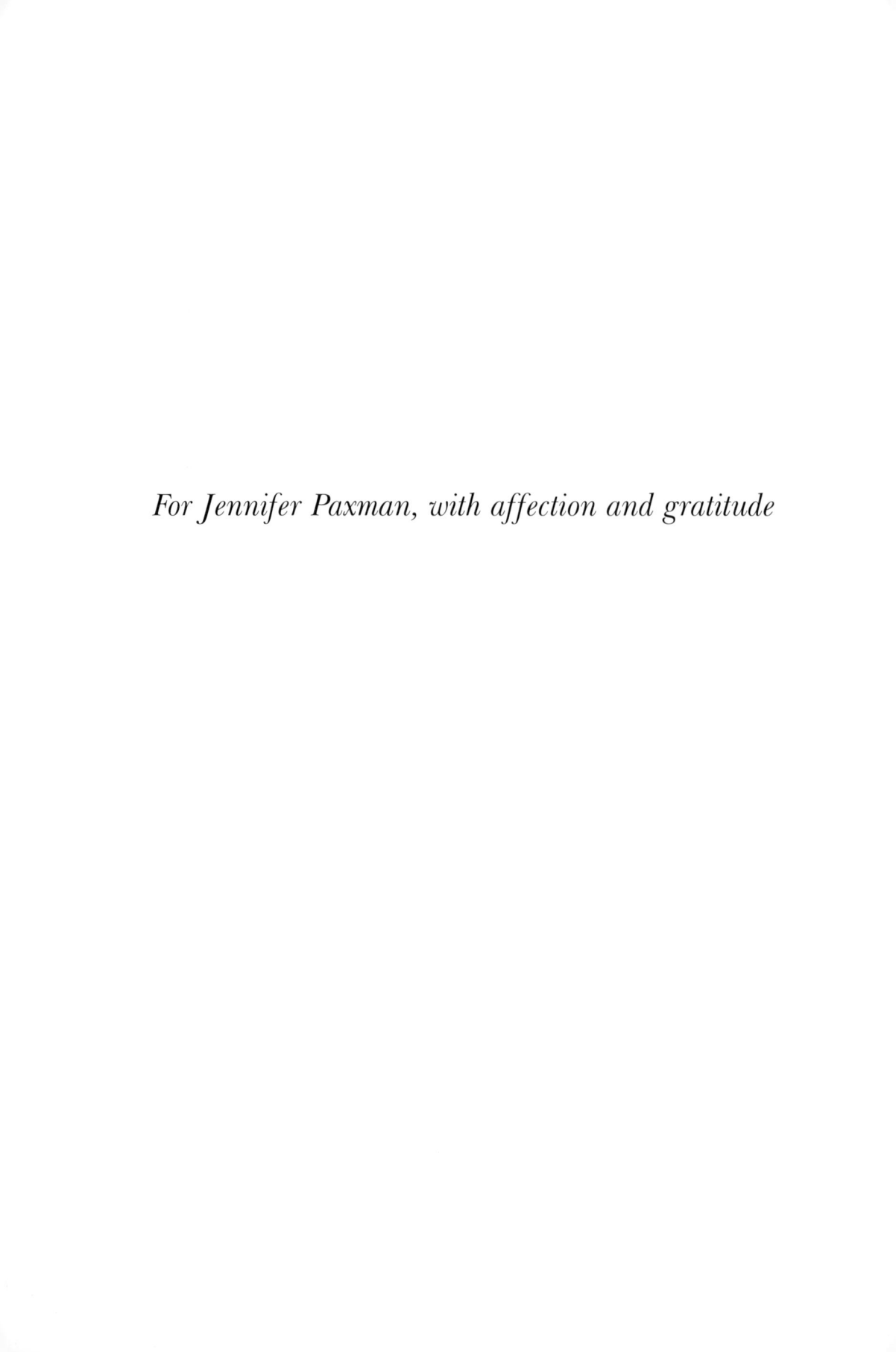

For Jennifer Paxman, with affection and gratitude

Andrew H. Morton

BREWIN BOOKS

First published by
Brewin Books Ltd, 56 Alcester Road,
Studley, Warwickshire B80 7LG in 2009
www.brewinbooks.com

© Andrew H. Morton 2009

All rights reserved.

ISBN: 978-1-85858-455-3

The moral right of the author has been asserted.

A Cataloguing in Publication Record
for this title is available from the British Library.

Typeset in Baskerville
Printed in Great Britain by
Hobbs the Printers Ltd.

CONTENTS

Acknowledgements	vi
Introduction	vii
1. Tolkien and Worcestershire	1
2. Bag End Farm	8
3. J.R.R. Tolkien and Bag End	17
4. Jane Neave at Dormston	27
5. The Name Bag End	34
Appendix	41
Recommended Reading	56
Index	58

ACKNOWLEDGEMENTS

Jennifer Paxman for permission to publish Brookes-Smith family photographs and her advice on Jane Neave and others. Maggie Burns for her advice and information on the Suffield family. The Rev Nick Wright of Inkberrow for introducing me to Miss Marian Collins of Dormston and Mrs Alison Green, both of whom helped clarify my perspective on Bag End. Thanks also to Miriam Tilt for her archive material on the Kington and Dormston Women's Institute. The Worcester County Records Office for their help and also their permission to publish photographs from their archive. I appreciate the advice of Wayne Hammond and Christina Scull on various Tolkien-related questions. Finally, thanks to Dr Della Hooke for putting me right on a couple of medieval matters.

INTRODUCTION

When I was researching my book *Tolkien's Gedling 1914* in 2007, I was generously given a little photo album concerning Jane Neave's time at Bag End. This tiny album, lovingly bound and consisting of fifteen small Box Brownie photographs was entitled *Aunt Jane's Little Book of Bag End* and it immediately started me thinking about gathering together what information I could about the Worcestershire farm that famously gave its name to the distinguished abode of Bilbo and Frodo Baggins in J.R.R. Tolkien's *The Hobbit* and *The Lord of the Rings*.

By this time I had conceived a great interest in Tolkien's influential aunt Jane Neave, and was in the process of building the short biography that appears in my Gedling book. My main informant in that process was Jennifer Paxman, whose family, the Brookes Smiths, enjoyed a friendship with Jane Neave that lasted over three generations and fifty years. Her father, Colin Brookes Smith, had written two interesting Tolkien related memoirs, and the photographs Jennifer gave me were taken by him, some time between 1923 and 1931 during family visits to Bag End. They are not professional photographs, just family snaps, yet their casual quality endows them with a certain charm. They present us with an oblique view into the Tolkien background, but at least they are a way of starting to explore the significance of Bag End Farm about which very little has been written. I originally saw this book, as a kind of pictorial account with the snaps of Bag End as the core of interest. Since then an exploration of local archives and a few visits to Dormston and people associated with the place have unearthed more material which I hope will be of interest.

The approach I have taken in this short book is similar to the one I adopted in the writing of *Tolkien's Gedling 1914*, that is, to take a small but significant part of the Tolkien background and to give it more attention than it has so far been afforded by the major biographers. In doing so, my aim has been to explore and reveal material which might cast some new light on Tolkien's writing. Both books started with a kernel of intriguing facts to do with names, places and people, which I explored until I was satisfied that something original had emerged. In both cases, I hope that I have been able to include material that either gently corrects or, in a small way, adds to what we know about the biographical context of Tolkien's writing. There is a limited amount of duplication between the two books, particularly because both of them partly concern Tolkien's influential aunt Jane Neave and Tolkien's Suffield family background. I have attempted to keep this to the minimum whilst at the same time keeping both books free-standing.

For those who come across this story for the first time, here is a quick résumé: J.R.R. Tolkien's favourite aunt, Jane Neave (nee Suffield) bought a farm at Dormston, near Inkberrow in Worcestershire, possibly in late 1922, but more probably in 1923. The farm was called Bag End. Her period of residence corresponds with the time that Tolkien was beginning to formulate the stories that later became *The Hobbit*, and Tolkien incorporated the name of the farm in his fiction as the home of Bilbo and, subsequently, Frodo Baggins. That, in a way, is the whole story and there's not a lot to it. Tolkien visited Bag End at least twice and possibly on more occasions, but there is no documentary record of these visits, and he has virtually nothing to say on the subject.

This may sound like a rather slight basis for a book but much of what has been written to date has been skimpy, misleading or downright erroneous, so I considered this my opportunity to write something substantial about an admittedly minor aspect of the Tolkien background. As with my previous book, I expect it to be of interest to serious Tolkien fans and also those with an interest in the local Worcestershire history.

Apart from the pictorial record, I have attempted to forge a context for Bag End in Tolkien's fiction: one general area of interest, about which the author does have something to say, is his profound attachment to the county of Worcestershire – the ancestral home of his maternal Suffield family; I have written on the name Bag End, its origin and resonance in Tolkien's fiction; the farm itself as well as its history are also examined in some detail; finally I have something to say about Jane Neave herself before, during and after her eight year stay at Bag End.

Throughout I have tried to balance the factual side of this book with reasonable speculation. Where factual information is thin on the ground it has proved necessary to make some educated guesses.[1] It may well be that there is further research to do in Tolkien's unpublished correspondence concerning his visits to Bag End, but informed opinion tells me that any such correspondence is unlikely to exist, or, if it does, to be of a fairly humdrum nature. This doesn't change the fact that it would be wonderful to have at least one photograph of Tolkien at Bag End; one may exist somewhere, but it has to be said that it was Hilary Tolkien's family and the Brookes Smiths who formed the close circle around Jane rather than her nephew Ronald, who was not always in touch.

Finally, I would like to make it clear that this is a book about Bag End in the 1920s and the early part of the twentieth century. The current owners of the house and farm, having bought it before all the Tolkien interest began, are understandably concerned about their privacy and I would strongly urge the curious to respect this. How the house and land may have changed since Jane Neave's day is not my concern here, and I have resisted all temptations to indulge in casual snooping.

For the visitor to Dormston, there isn't really very much to see. The church of St Nicholas is rather picturesque on the outside, although generally unadorned on the inside apart from Jane Neave's slightly incongruous plaster plaque. Nearby Moat Farm can be seen from the lane running west from the church and is a very fine example of timber frame construction. Nothing much can be seen of Bag End – just the main gates and a few glimpses from the lane. I doubt whether anything terribly exciting ever happened there in the past, the present or the future for that matter but it is a pleasant place, quietly atmospheric and redolent of a certain kind of English past.

---

[1] Particularly with reference to the likely nature of the centuries-long refashioning of Bag End. I have had to base my account on logic and observation and the little documentary information that Jane Neave gives.

x

Chapter One
TOLKIEN AND WORCESTERSHIRE

Tolkien's letters mention several times the special affection he held for Worcestershire, which, barring the fact he happened to be born in South Africa, was effectively his home county. Surprisingly, he makes the mistake of saying that the hamlet of Sarehole, where he spent the happiest years of his childhood, was in Warwickshire. In fact, his early homes in Kings Heath, Moseley and Sarehole were all in Worcestershire. Rednal too, where the Tolkien brothers and their mother stayed from time to time before and after their mother's death, was in Worcestershire, and the land where he loved to roam, just south of the city of Birmingham, the area between Kings Heath, Kings Norton and what is now the M42 was, and still is, a remarkably scenic corner of that county despite its proximity to the city. Tolkien made several early watercolours of that landscape and the views he painted of The Lickey Hills and of Kings Norton from Bilberry Hill [1] are still largely unchanged today. When his mother died, she was buried at Bromsgrove, which no doubt would have cemented his relationship with the county even more strongly. Those whose ideas of Birmingham are coloured by those frightful views from the M6 might be surprised to see the pleasant tree-lined suburbs of the south and west of the city, suburbs which in Tolkien's day melted effortlessly into the lovely Lickey Hills and Clent Hills. Even when he lived briefly in the borders of slum-ridden Ladywood, Tolkien was never more than a short walk to suburban parks or a short tram ride to pleasant countryside. Much of the suburban development which now rings Birmingham was then a few decades in the future.

---

[1] *J.R.R. Tolkien Artist and Illustrator* – Wayne Hammond and Christina Scull.

Although the city of Worcester and towns like Droitwich, Kidderminster and Evesham are generally unremarkable, the Worcestershire countryside is often lovely with its wide skies, its gently rolling landscape, and its picturesque villages with their churches, pubs and cricket pitches. It is slightly out of the way, on the road to nowhere in particular except mid-Wales and possibly Birmingham, and it was, and still is a rural county, largely devoid of conspicuous wealth, subject to the whims of agricultural markets. In the 1920s and 1930s, the county was hit hard by an agricultural depression, and it would have had its share of poverty, which may explain Tolkien's use of the word "squalid" below. Worcestershire has none of the wealth and swagger of the Cotswold counties; it is not so well manicured but has an unpretentious appeal all of its own. It is, of course, the home of the long-running radio drama The Archers, and its fictional location, Ambridge, is based on Inkberrow, just two miles down the road from Dormston. To this extent, Worcestershire has not only a place in Tolkien's affection, but in the hearts of millions of radio listeners.

Tolkien said that there was no corner of that county, "however fair or squalid",[2] where he did not feel at home, and part of this feeling derived from his strong identification with his maternal Suffield family. He has only a little to say about his ancestral German roots, "which must long ago have become pretty thin" but makes it absolutely clear that he was a Worcestershire Suffield "by tastes, talents and upbringing".[3] As a scholar of old Germanic languages, he was rather disappointed that the Tolkiens didn't even have a smattering of their ancestral language. Like the Suffields, the Tolkiens were relatively prosperous trades people who had experienced their ups and downs. Various Tolkien relatives were important to the young J.R.R. Tolkien, but it was from the Suffields that he derived his distinctive characteristics.

In the 1890s, his branch of the extensive Suffield clan, headed by his grandfather, the redoubtable John Suffield, lived in Ashfield Road in Kings Heath. John Suffield was an enterprising man, typical of the family as a whole, and had owned a wholesale drapery business in the previous decade. In the mid 1890s, he had a partnership in a Birmingham iron foundry and also appears to have been a sales representative for the recently invented

---

[2] Letters, p.54.
[3] Letters p.54.

Jeyes Fluid. The family were not rich, but reasonably prosperous [4] in their pleasant Birmingham suburb. John Suffield was an imposing presence in many ways, a local personality known for his active membership of intellectual associations, his Unitarian preaching and his penchant for travel. He was a skilled draftsman, a bit of an artist [5] and an irrepressible writer of doggerel. It may be that these artistic, intellectual and literary traits found a genetic path into his grandson, whose art and poetry showed similar naïve enthusiasm. His daughter, Mabel, Tolkien's mother, was similarly gifted, and we know that it was her linguistic and artistic gifts that started Tolkien's abiding interest in languages and art.[6] Also present in the Ashfield Road house was his aunt (Emily) Jane, at that time a teacher in the King Edwards Bath Row School, who had just embarked on a science degree at Birmingham's Mason College, the forerunner of Birmingham University. She was engaged to the lodger, insurance inspector Edwin Neave, a match not entirely welcomed by her father. More of Jane later.

John Suffield liked to make much of his Worcestershire roots, even going as far as claiming a connection with Lord Suffield of that county. The aristocratic connection is highly unlikely, but he was right at least in asserting the proud pedigree of his family. The Suffields went back several generations in the district of Evesham known as Bengworth, where they had connections with the printing and publishing trade. They were on the top rung of the artisan ladder. Some of the family were certainly highly literate craftsmen at least, and a copy of Sterne's *Sentimental Journey*, signed "Sam Suffield, Bengworth 1789", shows that intellectual traditions in the family went back a long way. There is little doubt that the young Tolkien would have been made aware of these family traditions by the imposing Victorian patriarch and that they were instrumental in laying the foundations of his attachment to the county of Worcestershire. The

---

[4] When the family had flown the nest, they employed a live-in servant. John Suffield's subsequent house in Cotton Lane shows a clear increase in prosperity.

[5] At least one of his illustrations for a Christmas card was clearly the inspiration for one of the illustrations for The Hobbit. This picture, which bears a strong similarity to Tolkien's picture of Laketown, was shown to Maggie Burns by Oliver Suffield. It is a part of the Suffield Family Collection. Maggie's article on the subject is so far unpublished, but her discovery will no doubt make fascinating reading.

[6] The ability to draw was considered part of an all-round education in the 19th and early twentieth centuries. This was particularly so in Birmingham where hundreds of anonymous artists were employed creating designs for the city's metal products.

Suffields considered themselves exiled from their roots in their little suburban villa, an experience of deracination common in the upheaval of the nineteenth century for many English people. They made the best of their life in Birmingham, a progressive city with many opportunities for the industrious, but at heart they were Worcestershire people.

When he came to study Middle and Old English at Oxford in his early twenties, Tolkien claims, perhaps a little improbably, to have found an immediate affinity with the Middle English of the West Midlands and the older Mercian dialect of Old English. There is really no linguistic basis for this, except, perhaps, for a few dialect words, broad pre-modern vowel sounds or the hint of a soft burr known to linguists as the "post-vocalic R", typical of all western dialects from Worcestershire to Cornwall; what we do sense here, however, is a strong emotional identification with the West Midlands: Tolkien wanted to feel that affinity, even if it was partly fanciful.

In a letter to his son Christopher, written during 1945, Tolkien goes even further down this romantic road, telling his son that he is a descendant of the Hwicce people,[7] whose Dark Age territory stretched up from the Severn estuary to Worcestershire. There is clearly a strong tribal feeling there as well as the linguistic one and whatever the basis for these ideas, it seems that Tolkien's idea of Englishness and of his own identity find imaginative expression in his attachment to the West Midlands, and Worcestershire in particular. Language, ancestry and the region itself melded together in a way typical of his imagination.

In a 1955 letter to his American publisher, Tolkien describes himself as "a West-Midlander at home only in the counties upon the Welsh Marches". Although it is a fair way to Wales from Worcester, it is true that in the Dark Ages and the Middle Ages, this county was vulnerable to Welsh incursions. The boundaries between Saxon and Celtic Britain were less clearly defined. On the other hand, as Tolkien would have been well aware, Welsh princes and Mercian earls sometimes formed alliances against Danes or Northumbrians. In pre Conquest days, when kings held court at Worcester, we can imagine a variety of tongues spoken in this marginal land, the Mercian and Wessex dialects of English, Welsh, and perhaps even Norman French.[8] It was a mixed culture of different races and tongues and when we

---

[7] Letters, p.108.
[8] Normans were present in this part of the country in significant numbers prior to The Conquest.

look at the historical record of personal names connected with Dormston, we find people of English, Welsh and Scandinavian origin as well as their Norman overlords.[9] Perhaps this area where the ancient races met, contributed something to Tolkien's Middle Earth, which is characterised by the meeting of languages, races and customs.

From the top of the Malvern Hills, which are clearly visible from Bag End, the view looks one way into the unspectacular English shires and the other way across Herefordshire into mysterious Wales. For those who do not know the area, The Malvern Hills are the most spectacular geographical feature of Worcestershire and the towns of Great Malvern, Little Malvern and Malvern Wells, which cling to the sides of the hills, were fashionable resorts in the 19th century, attracting a host of celebrity visitors and residents. The hills, rising to 1500 feet, are often to be seen in a bluish, purplish haze, but in the right cyclonic conditions you can see as far as The Black Mountains and the Severn Estuary. So, although quintessentially English, Worcestershire is touched from a distance by Celtic magic. This kind of sensitivity to places and their ancient associations fuelled Tolkien's imagination: he was always preoccupied with the link between man and his landscape. To C.S. Lewis, who was a pupil at Malvern College before WW1, and to J.R.R. Tolkien , the Malvern Hills were a place of some significance and on more than one occasion they walked there in the company of George Sayer, an ex-student of Lewis's and confidant of Tolkien. This very picturesque landscape, the setting of the poem *Piers Plowman*, and the site of ancient mythical battles (it was said that the British Camp saw the last stand of Caractacus against the Romans) was clearly a stimulant not only to the imagination of Lewis, who conceived the beginning of *The Lion the Witch and the Wardrobe* [10] there, but also to Tolkien with his sensitivity to the English landscape. You cannot stand at the summit of the Malvern Hills without sensing some spectacular and heroic whispers of the past The Welsh Marches were an evocative place for Tolkien whose fiction and fictional languages embody elements of English and Celtic traditions.

---

[9] 174v Great Domesday Book is claimed on this strange document on the National Archive site. Clearly Domesday is not the origin of this list, but the names that I can identify do make sense, and I am prepared to give it some credence. For those interested, here is the URL: http://www.national archives.gov.uk/documentsonline/details-result.asp?Edoc_Id=7577716&queryType=1& resultcount=1805

[10] Occasioned by the apparition of an improbable isolated lamppost – they can still be seen.

John Suffield's mythologizing of his ancestral county may have borne fruit when two of his descendants returned to their roots to farm in the county. His grandson Hilary Tolkien, who was an able horticulturalist, acquired a fruit farm in Blackminster near Evesham and his daughter Jane Neave, long a widow in 1923, bought Dormston Manor Farm, otherwise known as Bag End. In his final decade (he lived to be 97 and died in 1930) John spent much of his time at Bag End with Jane, whom he probably always had in mind as the youngest daughter who would look after him in his old age. He must have felt a sense of homecoming during his visits to Bag End, and the picture we have of him looking out of the south doorway of the rambling manor house with his long white beard has a certain proprietary air.

So two of the Suffields returned to Worcestershire proper and farmed the land. Records of J.R.R. Tolkien at Hilary's fruit farm are sketchy, and of his visits to his Aunt Jane at Bag End virtually non existent, but it is certain that he visited Bag End at least twice in the 1920s, and that it was the habit of Jane to surround herself with friends and family. The Brookes-Smith family, with whom Jane had farmed in Nottinghamshire, and who continued a close relationship with her for fifty years, were certainly regular visitors in the 1920s, and the photographic record that exists in this book comes from their family archive. It is, perhaps, fair to imagine a free and easy coming and going of friends and family, Tolkiens, Brookes-Smiths and Suffields throughout this period. But as well as the name itself, there are features of Bag End and its location that may well have suggested material for his fiction. In his imagined Shire it would have been the most natural thing for him to incorporate elements of the countryside he knew and loved from his childhood and now, in his thirties, had reason to revisit. Tolkien is nothing if not picturesque, and his imagined landscapes, just as much as his stirring narratives, account for his great popularity.

If we are prepared to leave county boundaries a little blurred, and extend Tolkien's idea of the Welsh Marches to the surrounding counties, with Worcestershire at its heart, it is indisputable that this corner of England was, in the early 20th century, capable of inspiring great artistic achievement. It is where the homely English trait in our heritage comes face to face with the ancient and mysterious Celtic element of romance.

Bag End from the south side. This side of the house was refashioned long after the Elizabethan rebuilding. The large bricks and characteristic English bond brickwork suggest a much later date, perhaps late 18th or early 19th century. However, the chimneys are certainly original and whatever changes to the façade have taken place do not destroy the overall rambling charm of the building.

A poor quality print taken from the garden gate which nevertheless shows some more detail of the frontage of the house. The path is lined with sunflowers, a favourite of Jane's.

This thumbnail of Bag End – here "Bag Inn" is from a 1731 estate map. This is almost certainly a clerical error or a mishearing. On the map, which shows the strips of land worked by various named local farmers, Bag End is shown in isolation, unattached to any land in particular. This may suggest its principal status as a dwelling before the enclosure of 1791 after which it may have more clearly defined as a farmhouse. The view is from the north.

The cattle pond to the south east of the farmhouse showing, on the right, one of the workshops and, behind the trees on the left, one of the elaborate dovecotes. The farm was principally pasture in Jane Neave's day with only a quarter of the land devoted to arable farming. These ponds may have been fed by a spring, but more likely the Winterbourne stream which in those days formed the eastern boundary of the farm. It may be that the two pools were a remnant of the original moat.

A glowing, slightly over-exposed view along the east side of the house by the cattle yard. One of Jane's dogs can be seen in the background (species unidentified). The east side of the house was the business end of Bag End, facing, as it did, the cattle yard and the main farm buildings.

This shot of the south east corner of Bag End shows again that it is more practically orientated than the more elegant west wing. It is also somewhat lower than the rest of the house. The fine studded door is almost certainly original, but the windows, including the dormers are probably of a later date than the original house.

Another view of the house from the south east. If you went out from this cattle gate you would see the main western entrance to Bag End with its impressive double gates, leading from the lane.

Jane Neave with another one of her dogs, Dak. Jane, who was somewhat camera-shy, was very often photographed with a dog. Here in her mid to late fifties, we see Jane in the typical no-nonsense practical clothing of a lady farmer. Her strong features are full of character, the face handsome and strong in contrast to the finer features of her sister Mabel.

VI

Jane's father, Tolkien's grandfather, John Suffield, here in his nineties. John spent much time with Jane at Bag End, although he always retained his house in Cotton Lane, Moseley. John Suffield, a daunting Victorian patriarch, influenced the intellectual and artistic development of the whole family, including Tolkien himself. His death, at the age of 97 in 1930, may have been a factor in Jane's selling the farm in 1931.

A view of the south west corner of Bag End. Jane was fond of the typically Elizabethan little leaded window on the left. This picture shows something of the house's construction – the brick in-filling and the double strength timber on the lower level to support the massive brick construction.

VII

Two views of the elaborate Elizabethan over mantels that graced the house. Wood panelling was a necessity in timber-framed houses as a form of insulation. Tolkien's fictional Bag End also features wood panelling, and perhaps the Dutch tiles of the hearth remind us of the chequered floor of Bilbo's house.

The top picture of the drawing room and shows the elaborate fireplace and over mantel design. Below this is the hall which formed the central portion of the main building. On the far right, (the west side) behind a screen can be seen the entrance to the staircase.

VIII

A view of Bag End in the early 1900s which makes clear the situation of the workshops and dovecotes. Here the usually impressive west entrance to Bag End seems to be littered with cut branches, but in Jane Neave's day, it was kept in an impressively tidy state. It is probable that Jane took a very real interest in the aesthetic as well as the practical side of the farm.

Here in a picture of around 1900, and looking a little neglected, is the original Elizabethan staircase. It had two short flights of stair and no well but featured impressive tall, moulded "vases" on the newel posts. Jane enjoyed such features, many of which, similar or identical, were typical of other prestigious manor houses of that period.

Perhaps the three cathedrals of Gloucester, Worcester and Hereford, with their great musical tradition have something to do with the association of several of our greatest composers with the area; of course, there is Elgar, but also Vaughan Williams and Holst,[11] Ivor Gurney and Herbert Howells, who also have roots there. In their music there is something deeply nostalgic but also something which is a sublime expression of Englishness. Yet theirs was not a facile lyricism and a disturbing current of true modernism flows in all of them just below the surface. It is the same strand of modernity that runs through the poetry of Housman and Gurney and Edward Thomas,[12] whose last poem composed in England, was written on the nearby summit of May Hill in Gloucestershire. In their evocation of the English pastoral, these poets and musicians are deeply aware of the troubling undercurrents of the modern world, of war, social upheaval and the end of a certain kind of England. Tolkien himself was not a modernist in the same sense, preferring traditional forms, but it is undoubtedly the case that his writing is informed by a deep insecurity about the modern world with its attendant horrors of war, ideology, industrialization and the despoiling of the English countryside. Much of Tolkien's writing is light-hearted and purely entertaining, but when he hits those deeper notes in his fiction, everything totters on the brink of destruction and an inexorable process of entropy is at work in the world. These ideas are never far from the surface and, if we are to understand his work as in any way modern or relevant to our own times, it is in this sense. Whatever real-life geographical home is claimed for The Shire, it is undeniable that in his imagination, that place is partly an evocation of his beloved Worcestershire.

---

[11] Although both born in Gloucestershire, Vaughan Williams' and Holst's composing careers are not subsequently associated with this area, except in their association with The Three Choirs.
[12] Famously in August 1914 the American poet Robert Frost and Edward Thomas holidayed at Ledbury and it was here that Thomas first took poetic inspiration from the landscape.

Chapter Two

BAG END FARM

Bag End, otherwise known as Dormston Manor Farm, in its present form dates from 1582, when it was substantially rebuilt by John Russell, probably with a view to its lease or sale.[1] That is more or less the house that Jane Neave owned during the 1920s, and a detailed description of the house at that time follows later in this chapter. It is variously known as Bag-End, Bag End, Bagend, Bag-End Farm and Bag End Farm as well as Manor Farm, Dormston Manor Farm and just plain Dormston Manor.

However, as Jane Neave mentions in her sales brochure of 1931,[2] it is more than likely that there was a previous manor house or houses on the site before this date; one can only guess at what was there but it was probably another timber framed building on a smaller scale. Although the term "manor" is Norman in origin, this feudal administrative term merely rationalises what was already there in Anglo-Saxon times, and when a tenth century charter of King Edgar mentions "Deormodesealdtune" (Deormod's old enclosure) it is reasonable to conclude that the settlement and its principal residence had been there from earlier times. However, it may be that Dormston at that time was more of a village (later depopulated) and that there was no associated manor house.

Whatever form the house took in these days, before and after the Norman conquest, is unknown, but it was certainly different from the Elizabethan rebuilding. It was this earlier house that was acquired by John Russell of Strensham [3] in 1388. He immediately applied for "license to

---

[1] See Jane Neave's "Historical Notes" in the appendix.
[2] WCRO – Ref: 2919 – included in its entirety as an appendix to this book.
[3] Master of the King's Horse.

crenellate" at Dormston and at his principle residence at Strensham, a license granted by Richard II in that year. Although "license to crenellate" seems to suggest permission to add fortifications, in effect such a licence was more a matter of prestige indicating a favourable relationship with and loyalty to the overlord, in this case, the king. However, in these lawless times, when disputes between the gentry and gentry and landowners and the common people were always likely to spill over into violence, it is likely that the original manor house had some elements of fortification. The late 14th century was a troubled time and the kind of local disputes that were likely to arise would justify some element of defensibility as a deterrent if nothing else. This may have merely taken the form of a moat, traces of which can be detected around Bag End and which exist in a clearer form at Moat Farm.

The Russells of Strensham were lords of the manor from 1388 to 1705 when their line effectively petered out. They were substantial land owners in Worcestershire and elsewhere throughout this period, significant movers and shakers in the political life of the country, and it seems unlikely that they would have chosen to live in this isolated location. No Russells appear in parish records, and anyway, Dormston was then, as it is now, an out-of-the-way place, which is not even marked on the Saxton map of 1577 or the Speed map of 1610. But when another John Russell had Bag End rebuilt in 1582, he did an impressive job, and many of the features of the house suggest a country residence of high status. In the previous century, the two large dovecotes, one of which is clearly dated 1413, suggest something of the seigniorial status of Bag End. Strict rules circumscribed the right to build dovecotes and the ones at Bag End were of impressive size, comprising between 500 and 600 nests.[4]

Born in 1551, the Sir John Russell (knighted in 1587), who was responsible for the rebuilding of Bag End, had a colourful, troubled and disputatious career. Combining the roles of Justice of the Peace, Sheriff, Escheator [5] and Deputy Lieutenant of the shire, he was involved in a lengthy dispute with his Catholic wife and father-in-law, during which he threatened to disinherit his own children. This kind of religious schism

---

[4] Mrs Alison Green, who lived at Moat Farm in the 1950s, a farm which also had a dovecote, mentions interestingly that the number of nests was always odd, a fact probably explained by the arrangement of the nesting holes on adjacent rows. This curious fact, which I have no reason to doubt, may deserve some future research.

[5] In the role of Escheator, he was in a position to keep an eagle eye on all property in the county.

within a family was a common feature of the period with some members of the landed classes holding on to their old Catholic faith and others conforming to the new religious order. But John Russell was no mere conformist: a strong protestant and a peevish and warlike man, he was constantly in trouble with the authorities, despite his official roles, and his squabbles sometimes boiled over into violent action. But like other major landowners of the time who had benefited from the new regime, he took great care with the consolidation of his estates, and we see the evidence of that in the impressive rebuilding of Bag End. The Bag End of 1582 was a very large and impressive manor house and whoever lived there enjoyed a privileged life-style and considerable manorial rights. In her "Historical Notes" Jane has the house let or sold to Richard Cholmeley and Richard Buller, surnames which occur frequently in local records indicating middle-ranking gentry. The Cholmelys were related by marriage to the Russells and Richard Buller appears to have been an M.P. after 1604, so these were fairly important people.

The Bag End that Tolkien knew in the 1920s represented several layers of history. It is certain that the picturesque outbuildings including the dovecotes, which by this time had been put to more practical use as tool shed and garage, date from the fifteenth century. The west and south wings can be confidently dated to 1582, although how much of a previous building might have been incorporated is unclear. The south-facing main aspect of the building appears to have been rebuilt entirely of brick at a later date . The business end of the farm – the east wing – may not have been a part of the original Elizabethan building but a later addition indicating a change from primarily residential to agricultural use.

The appendix at the end of this book, which presents in full Jane Neave's 1931 sales brochure, gives a detailed account of the internal lay-out of Bag End, but it will be of interest to expand a little on this account, especially in the light of more recent changes to the farm.

Contemporary maps and aerial photographs show that the main access to Bag End is now by way of a made-up road which leads at an angle back from the vicinity of the church. Although maps from Jane Neave's time show paths following roughly the same route, this recent addition is clearly to facilitate the movement of modern farm machinery, none or little of which was employed on the farm in the 1920s. However, Jane does say that one of the outbuildings had been converted into a garage, and it is conceivable that at least one tractor was at work here in the 1920s, so the unmade track leading back from the church may have started to assume a more important function. Jane certainly owned a car in later years, and may have at this date.

The main access in the 1920s was from the lane which leads from the main road to the church; the impressive double gates are still there and photographs of the time show them clearly in use. This western approach probably dates from a post-enclosure date (1791) when the main aspect of the house was changed from north to south facing. In her sales brochure of 1931, "frontage to a good road" is mentioned as a selling point. At the time this western approach to the house was pleasantly landscaped and would have given a rather grand impression. The photographs in the 1931 sales brochure show that the grounds in front of the house were neatly kept. The visitor would walk fifty yards or so between the three orchards, Walk Orchard with its pool, Perry Mill Orchard and House Orchard, before turning left to see the outbuildings on either hand and the main southern aspect of the house with its walled garden. Straight ahead was a cattle gate on the far side of which was another pool. This south or strictly speaking south-east facing aspect of the house was the main domestic entrance. However, Bag End being a working farm, the east wing, which faced the cattle-yard was, and still is, the business end of the building. It was plainer and more functional than the more picturesque west wing. In fact, this east wing may be a later addition, as Jane speculates in her sales brochure that the original house may have been of an L-shaped nature and have faced north. An estate map of 1731, referred to elsewhere in this book, shows that the east wing was in existence by that date, although the house as a whole does indeed face north. This original orientation to the north does make sense, as it would have faced the village, which in previous times had clustered round the church. This early map suggests that the east-west lane running through the village, past Moat Farm and the church, was the principle road at this time.

The elaborate wood panelling which characterises the grander rooms, especially the over mantels, are of real architectural interest and typical of the late Elizabethan and early Jacobean period. These fire surrounds and over mantels, with their imitation classical pillars and pilasters combined with cruder native motifs of squares, crosses and arches added a distinctive grandeur to the hearth – the focus of any room. They have a massive, slightly clumsy charm about them which falls short of later classical imitations. In her sales brochure, Jane Neave also points to the attractive nature of the main staircase. On a much smaller scale, these features bear a remarkable resemblance to those in Harvington Hall near Kidderminster, and the carpenters were clearly working to the same or similar patterns.

Half-timbered construction is a distinctive feature of the West Midlands generally, and as Bag End is a notable example, it is worth saying a few words about it. These houses have become emblematic of a certain kind of Englishness, superficially imitated in thousands of suburban dwellings in the modern era. Their decorative black and white fascias evoke images of a Merry England and a certain kind of imagined social order. In an England obsessive about property ownership everyone can be lord of the manor in their mock Tudor suburban semi. It is impossible to look at buildings like Bag End and Moat Farm without those associations. There are literally thousands of old timber framed buildings in this part of the country and they help to give it its distinctive picturesque quality. Moat Farm is a particularly fine example of timber frame construction; with its three storeys, it is arguably more aesthetically pleasing; Bag End with its later accretions is mixed in style but impressive for its size and the warm glow of brick between its massive timbers.

It may be that the availability of timber in this part of the world – here specifically from the ancient Feckenham Forest – has something to do with the prevalence of this kind of construction. Frames were assembled flat on the ground using mortis and tenon and dovetail joints; they were then disassembled when each timber had been numbered and put back together to make the building's framework, the joints reinforced with wooden pegs. The techniques of "scribe carpentry" were universal, but the end results, in terms of design, were very varied. The "squares" in the frame were filled in with wattle and daub, rubble, brick, plaster or a variety of media. In some cases, as with Moat Farm, the original haphazard in-filling was replaced over a period of time with brick as the old filling decayed or crumbled. Whatever the frames were filled with, being solid, they let in the cold; hence the extensive use of wood panelling in the interior.[6] The wood panelling at Bag End is certainly decorative and atmospheric, but it is also practical.

Expense and status was signified in the amount of timber used and the type of filling. A wattle and daub or rubble type filling was lighter and therefore the frame could be less massive. But in the case of a large house like Bag End, more timber was required, and the presence of more vertical timbers on the ground floor indicate a framework necessary to support a greater mass. Probably the 1582 rebuilding of Bag End involved the use of brick for the first time to make the house more substantial and prestigious. The historical record shows that all over Worcestershire, in the period following the dissolution of the monasteries, landowners were building in brick for the first time.[7] This could take two forms: either building from scratch in the new medium, or, more commonly encasing the older timber frame construction in brick. Bag End is likely to be one such hybrid building.[8] incorporating an older extant building into a more substantial brick-based project. The elaborate brick chimney stacks at Bag End date from this period and it is reasonable to suppose that the rest of the house followed suit. John Russell was certainly the kind of landowner and of the sort of social status to adopt this more prestigious kind of building.[9] But apart from the regular English bond pattern of the south facing frontage, apparently an 18th or early 19th century addition,[10] the brickwork is sometimes disorganised using different shapes and sizes of brick, and this may indicate that at least some of the brick infilling was gradually acquired over time and was not a feature of the 1582 rebuilding. As with Bag End in general, there is an ad hoc and slightly chaotic feel to it. Certainly in the case of the dovecotes, now in filled with brick, the use of this medium in 1413 would seem improbably early for original brick construction.

---

[6] When Englishmen moved to North America they found that the greater extremes of climate rendered the tradition English timber frame dwelling impractical.
[7] In the Elizabethan period we find local coal mining activity partly directed towards the firing of brick.
[8] On a much grander scale, Harvington Hall is another example of this encasing process.
[9] In doing this he would have been emulating John Packington, who is reputed to have rebuilt no fewer than thirty of his Worcestershire buildings in brick.
[10] This kind of improvement was common in the period. The sales brochure suggests that it was at this time that the main aspect of the house was changed from north to south. This change may well be linked to the 1791 enclosure, which saw the main road established for the first time.

An eighteenth century map shows that land in the Parish of Dormston was still farmed on the ancient strip farming basis, with various farmers owning elongated fields scattered across the whole area. On this map of 1731, the names of Callow,[11] Collins and Savage are predominant. Add to those the names of Poole and Vernon, and you have the whole cast of players who were involved in the 1791 [12] enclosure of the land. It was land that was the important thing rather than the dwellings, and these canny businesslike yeoman farmers bought and sold and haggled over it in a way that can still be pieced together from mountains of legal documentation. *The History of Worcestershire, Volume 4* presents us with a list of the owners of Bag End, or, a slightly different thing, the manor of Dormston, from the Norman Conquest. But what land and buildings were owned or tenanted and by whom is a question that can really only be answered when a modern pattern of ownership emerges in the 19th century. It is a massive subject and well outside the scope of this book, but the documentary evidence suggests that the list is not complete [13] and that more research could be done.

The Bag End Farm that Jane Neave bought in the early 1920s comprised just over two hundred acres, an area corresponding to roughly one quarter of all the land in Dormston parish.[14] Only a quarter of the land was arable, mainly to the south and east of the farm and the rest pasture. There were also substantial orchards near to the house and in the land surrounding the farm's two cottages. The name "Perry Mill Orchard" perhaps suggests that one of the farms products had been pear cider or perry. The presence of another Perry Mill Farm nearby confirms this typical cider making occupation. There were also two pools, one in the House Orchard and another fifty yards or so south of the farm, the purposes of which were the watering of cattle. To the north and west was Green's Wood, perhaps twenty acres of woodland. Aerial photographs show that today the field pattern is roughly the same, although more of the

---

[11] The initials IC 1663 for Iacobus Callow were inscribed on Moat Farm seventy years previously, a date which probably indicates a replastering job rather than the construction of the building.
[12] WCRO – Inclosure (sic) Ward Ref: 307/31.
[13] For example, a conveyancing document of 1733 shows a certain Robert Savage selling Bag End, a property he may have owned following the demise of the Russells in 1705. WCRO Deed of Conveyance Ref: 2219.
[14] Given as "five hides" in Domesday. Although a hide is a unit of taxation rather than area, the conventional estimate of 120 acres seems right here.

land is dedicated to arable than in Jane Neave's day. As Jane says,[15] "The land is sound and only a small proportion under the plough". Good pasture land was highly prized: you could plough it up in a day, but if you did so, it would take years to restore.[16] Like many dairy farmers, Jane loved her livestock, giving them elaborate and sometimes bizarre names, as in her previous farm in Nottinghamshire, which was always dominated by an impressive and diverse array of livestock.

To take on such a farm, at least twice the size of her combined Gedling farms, was a bold move but with ten years of practical farming experience behind her, she would have been up to the task. Jane favoured all-women partnerships, and until 1927, she shared the work with Marjorie Atlee, who had worked as a land-girl on the Gedling farms. As this was a legally constituted partnership (dissolved in 1927 when Marjorie married Jane's nephew Frank Suffield) it is likely that Marjorie bought into the enterprise. She was an ex-pupil of Jane's from Birmingham days, and, as a King Edward's pupil, is likely to have been comfortably middle-class. Apart from the photographs in this book, there is no record of her Bag End farming operation, unlike her Nottinghamshire enterprise, which I have documented elsewhere. However, we do know that she approached farming from a scientific and sometimes experimental standpoint, and the word-of-mouth accounts of her from older residents of Dormston, suggest that she was single-mindedly modern in her management of the farm. "She would have had her own ideas", Miss Marian Collins told me. Her father worked on an occasional basis for Jane Neave and there is a suggestion that this lady farmer may have shaken things up a little in the Dormston farming community.

Nothing less should be expected of the determined and enterprising Jane, and although she was eventually defeated by the severe agricultural depression that hit Worcestershire in the late 1920s, the contents of her 1931 sales brochure show an obvious pride in the farm and the house at Bag End. Economic conditions militated against the kind of investment the farm would have needed to turn it into an efficient modern operation. The existence of a garage may suggest that she had at least one tractor, but by and large farming in the 1920s was still un-mechanized, depending on intensive seasonal manual labour.

---

[15] See Appendix.
[16] The threat of ploughing up pasture was a weapon the tenant could use against the landowner.

Jane was intrepid, determined and businesslike. Her love of farming was founded in her scientific specialities of botany and physiology, but also, perhaps, in the Suffield family's romantic notion of a rural family past. But it is also clear that she took great pleasure and pride in her rambling manor house, which must have been something of a fulfilled dream for a woman whose roots went back to the pleasant but very ordinary suburbs of Birmingham. Certainly the rural surroundings of Dormston must have suited her, as she played a full part in community life until 1948, living at her modest cottage near the church.

Chapter Three

J.R.R. TOLKIEN AND BAG END

In a letter of 1968,[1] Tolkien wrote: "In the case of Bag-End, I did not invent it, it was, in fact, the local name for a house an aunt lived in in Worcestershire: an old tumbledown manor house at the end of an untidy lane that led nowhere else."[2]

You can scour the letters of J.R.R. Tolkien for hours looking for specific references to real places in his fiction and not come up with anything much. This vagueness, or obtuseness, depending on which way you look at it, has led to much speculation among those who, like myself, have a sense of the author's affinity with a certain kind of English landscape. But Tolkien may have had an instinct that to reveal too much about real topography would be to break the spell that his fiction weaves. Typically his responses to queries about the origin of names, places and persons in his fiction were politely vague, acknowledging the interest his fiction had stirred, but sticking to generalities. Sometimes he is helpful: the term hobbit may have been inspired in some way by Sinclair Lewis's *Babbit* but has nothing to do

---

[1] The letter in question is part of a reply to K. Jackson, who is asking permission to use the name Bag End. Tolkien also replies: "...it may interest you to know that (however unfair it may seem) it is impossible to patent mere names..." This oddly punctuated letter was partly reproduced and partly quoted in Sotheby's (London), *English Literature, History, Children's Books and Illustrations*, auction catalogue for 12 July 2005, p.246. It can be viewed on the Tolkien Library web site.

[2] Pictures of Bag End and its grounds show it far from "tumbledown", although its growth over the centuries led to a building that was not stylistically homogeneous. Maintenance may have been something of a nightmare, but Jane Neave always liked things "just so" and would not have tolerated anything chaotic if she could help it. The lane he is referring to must be the cut-back route from the church which may have been only semi-constructed in Jane's day If he arrived by taxi and the main gates were closed, he may well have been taken by the cut-back route, which would explain the "untidy lane". One can see that Tolkien may be playing with the "cul de sac" idea in defining the farm in this way.

with rabbits; sometimes he is dismissive, stating that some of his place names are simply nonsense; sometimes he is irritable when translators try him with queries about Dutch or Norwegian equivalents. Generally though, he contents himself with a vague formula, explaining, for example, that the Shire is based loosely on the English countryside and that hobbits are English rustic folk. What mattered to him was the status of *The Hobbit* and *The Lord of the Rings* as works of the imagination, and this, after all, is what mainly interests us. It is understandable that he should not want to tie himself down to specific sources in the real world. For Tolkien one suspects that this kind of discussion would be largely irrelevant and possibly somewhat irritating. Two phrases that Tolkien used to dismiss this kind of discussion were "private amusements" and "mere learned note"; I fear this book may fall into both categories.

Apart from the letter cited above, Tolkien has virtually nothing to say on the subject of Bag End, and this passing reference suggests that he attached no great significance to his use of the name or the place itself. Whatever there is to say about Bag End, this lack of authorial comment has left a rather intriguing blank space. The few comments that come from biographers about Jane's farm are either speculative or simply misguided. One respected biographer has Bag End as "a cottage", an assertion that is simply ludicrous and indicates this neglect.[3] In fact, Bag End was a substantial Elizabethan manor house of considerable historical interest over and above its Tolkien connection, and given Tolkien's enthusiasm for the kind of traditional Englishness it represented, I cannot see how it could have failed to figure in his imagination as he began to write *The Hobbit* around 1930. The germs of this story go back before this date, coinciding completely with the period of Jane's ownership.

Let me make it clear that I am not on some lunatic quest to prove that the fictional "Bag End" bore a close relationship to Jane Neave's farm. Ultimately one can only guess to what extent Tolkien had the real place in mind as he wrote the first pages of *The Hobbit*. However, it is in the nature of fantasy that the reader should interrogate the origin of ideas; intentionally or not, a writer like J.R.R. Tolkien invites this kind of speculation, looking for places or events that might have sparked some narrative element. It may be impertinent or irrelevant to do so, but it's all

---

[3] One Internet site shows a picture of Hill Farm in Dormston and bills it as Phoenix Farm!

a part of the game, and it's hard to resist. There are some well-attested real-life locations that influenced Tolkien – Sarehole Mill and the two towers of Edgbaston, for example – but what about Bag End? It is possible to argue that there are things about the real farm that bear a not-so-speculative resemblance to Bilbo Baggins' homely abode. I offer these ideas as speculation but speculation that is based in some kind of reality.

Perhaps it would make sense at this point to remind ourselves of the role that "Bag-End" (in *The Hobbit*) and "Bag End" (in *The Lord of the Rings*) plays in both books. It is an important location in as much as it is the starting and ending place of both stories and as such it is of essential importance. If Peter Jackson's film trilogy can be seriously criticised for anything, it would be the omission of the return to The Shire, a penultimate chapter in which the momentous events of the rest of the story find a disturbing resonance in the ordinarily unadventurous world of hobbits. Classic narratology theory informs us with some reason that all the great stories begin with an event which takes the hero from their everyday world and leads them on a perilous adventure, eventually to return in triumph to their starting place. This idea, which has become something of a Hollywood cliché (known as "the mythic content" by film moguls) is one that was consciously taken lock stock and barrel by George Lucas for his Star Wars saga. But it is also a pattern which Tolkien, with his extensive knowledge of folklore, would have encountered again and again. All the elements are there: the initially un-heroic hero, the great quest and the confrontation with evil, the faithful companion and the mysterious spirit guide. It could be argued that the deep and lasting appeal of *The Hobbit* and *The Lord of the Rings* stems from their adherence to this narrative pattern, in which "Bag End" fulfils the important role of home, the starting place and the terminus.

For J.R.R. Tolkien this initial fictional location of Bag End, with its homely comforts, must have had a particular importance. In his life, Tolkien, like his hobbit heroes, had no particular fondness for adventures and the only times that anything really exciting happened to him came close to ending in disaster, even death. One thinks of his disastrous trip to France where the mother of the two Mexican boys he was looking after died, his avalanche experience in the Alps in 1911, and his experiences on The Somme. In some ways the author's life was remarkably hobbit-like; he lived a rather humdrum suburban existence; he liked his pipe and his pint in the cosy ambience of the traditional pub; even his descriptions of himself are typically self-deprecating and ironic suggesting a body and a temperament unfit for heroic action.

It is at the beginning of *The Hobbit* that Bag-End is closest to a simple children's storybook location, and the opening pages of the book gives us a guided tour round Bilbo's desirable residence. Bilbo resents the disruption that Gandalf and the Dwarves bring to his ordered existence, but eventually his Tookish side shows as he undertakes his burgling mission. On his return to Hobbiton, having put the greater mythical world to rights, order and rights of ownership must be restored after his missing-presumed-dead status have led to wholesale plundering of Bag End. This pattern is roughly followed in *The Lord of the Rings*, although the petty feuding between the Bagginses and the Sackville Bagginses has a more sinister resonance than in *The Hobbit*. In this more grown-up book the avarice and envy of the Sackville Bagginses is exploited by the malice of Saruman, and Frodo returns to find The Shire a nightmarish picture of brutality, exploitation and senseless bureaucracy. The once idyllic Bag End has been virtually destroyed in the process, but again, in time is restored. In both books, this motif of the old settled order which is disrupted and needs to be restored must express Tolkien's own vision of a world order. His views, which represent a mixture of the traditional and the libertarian, can be found throughout his published letters and are implied in his fiction. It is natural that a writer whose life work was so firmly founded in a linguistic and literary past should find fault with a decadent and tawdry present. As with many writers, childhood experiences are formative and of lasting significance; for Tolkien it was the idyllic few years spent with his mother and brother near Sarehole Mill. Memories of that golden era at Sarehole, where he and his brother let their imaginations run wild in creative play, must be counted as the major inspiration for The Shire, Hobbiton and Bag End. Tolkien goes some way to making this idea explicit in later letters where typically he laments the encroachment of suburbia on this rural idyll.

But if we are prepared to allow ourselves to go beyond Sarehole and speculate on some more specific parallels between Jane Neave's Bag End and the fictional Bag End, what do we find?

For a start, there is the Worcestershire location. Given Tolkien's emphatic identification with his ancestral roots in this county, one can have little doubt that he had his heartland in mind when he concocted The Shire and Hobbiton. Hobbits bear a close resemblance to rustic English people, and their home is set in pleasant rolling, well cultivated, and civilised country like Worcestershire – lovely and quintessentially English without being too spectacular. Tolkien found inspiration for his fictional Shire place names from all over England, and they are sewn into the fabric of his fiction just as the real names of sewn into the fabric of rural England. They are often the kind of names that exist around Bag End – names like Morton Underhill, Morton Bagot,[4] Branden Brook, Roundhill Wood, Perry Mill and the numerous Berrows on and around Jane's farm. They are unremarkable English names, but they are exactly the kind of names that populate Tolkien's fiction. One decidedly interesting place name that can be found in the boundary clause of the Anglo Saxon charter is Eomæres medwo (Eomer's Meadow), a field which exists about a quarter of a mile to the west of Bag End. It is mentioned in the Anglo Saxon Charter Bounds, although it later became Omber's Meadow. Is it possible that Tolkien noticed this name and took it for the name of the chief Marshall of Riddermark and adopted son of Théoden? If Tom Shippey is right, and The Mark is in fact Mercia,[5] and the names of its inhabitants based on names in the Mercian dialect, there may be an argument for this. However, Tolkien would have known the name Eomer from Beowulf and the Anglo Saxon Chronicle, where he is cited as the ancestor of all the Mercian kings. Still, it is a Mercian name in a very Mercian location.

Many claims have been made for the origins of the topography of Tolkien's fiction in different parts of the British Isles – parts of Scotland and Ireland, Lancashire and The Forest of Dean are amongst these. They may well all have something to say for them and it is not my intention to dispute any such claim here. My object, however, is to suggest that the area around Bag End may also be worth considering. Tolkien's maps of The Shire and his illustration called *The Hill: Hobbiton – across-the Water* immediately strike me as bearing some topological similarity to the location of Dormston in

---

[4] Perhaps echoes of Frogmorton here. Like Frogmorton, Morton Underhill (another Tolkien name) lies to the east of Dormston. (The old surname "Throckmorton" is one that is associated with this part of the country.)
[5] *J.R.R. Tolkien Author of the Century*, pp.91–92.

relation to the A422 Stratford to Worcester Road, which, in The Shire, would be known as The East Road. Hobbiton, like Dormston is a scattered settlement leading to an upland eminence to the north of the road and is reached by a winding lane similar to the one the author envisaged. In addition, the fictional and the real Bag End both face southwards. Undoubtedly, the mill and the river in this illustration are based on the mill and the river at Sarehole, but the general topography of Hobbiton is far more like Dormston than Sarehole, which is low-lying. Again, there are parallels between Tolkien's map entitled *A Part of the Shire* and the area around Dormston, and the location of the settlements, the patches of woodland,[6] the place names, and the general lie of the land are open to such an interpretation if one is so minded. Perhaps they are just typical features of the English landscape, but it is possible that they were part of Tolkien's mental map when he came to write *The Hobbit*.

Jane Neave's Bag End was, of course, very far from the well-appointed hole in the ground that Tolkien describes. However, if you wanted to look further, there are a few features of the real Bag End that correspond in some way to the famous hobbit-hole.

The "Bag End"[7] Tolkien imagined was on one floor as opposed to the three of the real Bag End. But the real Bag End was a positive maze of rooms on the ground floor, ten in all, including a panelled inner hall, a study, a lounge, a back hall, a bathroom an inner hall, a dining room, a large and cool dairy, a kitchen and a store. This was a profusion of rooms that reminds one of Bilbo's well-appointed abode.[8] In John D. Rateliff's book *Mr Baggins*,[9] the author observes that "Some of the details of the description of Bag-End itself conjure up the civilised atmosphere of a comfortable sitting room in an old manor house…." Throughout his life, Tolkien lived in modest and relatively modern houses, if anything incongruously suburban. It is not unreasonable to suggest that when he came to the mental design of "Bag End" something on the scale and design of Jane Neave's farmhouse came to mind. "Bag End" combines two things

---

[6] Quartern Ash Wood, Roundhill Wood, Green's Wood and Upper Kite's Wood are all survivals of a continuous forest from Anglo Saxon times.
[7] In *The Hobbit* "Bag-End" and in *The Lord of the Rings* "Bag End".
[8] "…bedrooms, bathrooms, cellars, pantries (lots of these), wardrobes (he had a whole room devoted to clothes) kitchens, dining rooms…" The Hobbit – p.1.
[9] *Mr Baggins*, p.45.

that Tolkien valued – the domestic comforts and convenience of an ordinary home with something more picturesque and grand. It was the kind of rambling rule-of-thumb arrangement that would have appealed to Ronald's English aesthetic. From his times at King Edward's School and in Oxford, he was comfortably familiar with ancient oak panelled rooms of the statelier past, as he was later in the snug yet unplanned rooms of The Eagle and Child. But beneath the layers of added and adapted building at Bag End were layers of history emblematic of a very English past.

When Jane came to sell Bag End in 1931, the particulars she gives in an extensive sales-brochure describing the house and the land dwell on certain interesting features, and one can have little doubt that these would all have been proudly displayed to Tolkien when he visited.

One of the main features of Bag End was the extensive and elaborate oak panelling of the late Elizabethan era. We see nothing so elaborate in Tolkien's illustration entitled *The Hall at Bag End, Residence of B. Baggins Esquire* but Tolkien, on the opening page of *The Hobbit*, does mention panelled walls, and the illustration does indeed show wood panelling. Floors at "Bag End" were "tiled and carpeted". The floors on the ground floor of Bag End were flagged or part flagged, which is not quite the same thing, but the black and white tiles in Tolkien's illustration may have been suggested by the "Dutch tiled hearth" of the dining room, clearly visible in the photograph. In any case, flagged or part flagged suggest a combination of stone and carpeted floors.

There were no circular doors at Bag End, which is something of a disappointment. On the other hand, there were two massive ancient studded doors, on the south and east side of the building, of much the same kind of plank construction we see in Bilbo's home. It is possible that these doors belonged to an even earlier building than the Elizabethan manor house. Doors would have been reused in those days, along with other valuable wooden fixtures such as staircases and even floorboards. Although we have no colour photographs of these doors, it is most likely the front door at least was painted the traditional green. On the other hand, when we come to Bilbo's impressive "door furniture" Jane's brochure does make mention of a fascinating" oak door with original iron lock and hinges" which led to the wine store under the stairs. Finally, Jane did have a clock, a distinguished long-case clock which now resides in Australia. Unfortunately, the clock in Tolkien's illustration is of another variety, but "Uncle Ronald" once told a teenage fan [10] that there was a problem fitting a long case clock into a tunnel-shaped dwelling. So the clock was, and wasn't the clock in question. Also to be seen on the wall to the left of Bilbo's door is a barometer, not a remarkable item in itself, although Jane Neave did own a particularly fine barograph, possibly a wedding present from Bishop E.A. Knox to Jane and Edwin. Long case clocks and barometers are common items, but these were prized possessions of Jane at Bag End, and it is possible that when Tolkien came to visualize the interior of "Bag End", they found a natural place in its interior design.

One might add a little about the status of Bag End Farm in Dormston: like Bilbo's home, it was a cut above the rest, the kind of place that would excite pride of ownership, well appointed and possibly an object of mild envy – definitely "des res" in a quirky, old fashioned way. Mrs Green, who lived at the arguably more picturesque Moat Farm at a later date, was in no doubt that Bag End was the house of highest status in Dormston. It was, in fact, "the big house". In *The Hobbit* and *The Lord of the Rings*, "Bag End" is a residence that excites envy. Bilbo and Frodo are aloof from the kind of social climbing and snobbery that surround them in the world of The Shire – they are simply well-off, appreciating the good things in life, but they are also the focus of envy. Part of Tolkien's charm is his wicked codification of competitive middle-class attitudes and pretensions. Jane Neave was certainly not a snob, but she was always confident of her own worth and it is possible that her status as the owner of Dormston's principle residence, Bag End, which she would have kept in fine condition, suggested certain parallels with the leading position of the Bagginses in Hobbiton.

Apart from these details, it is possible to argue that the rustic charm of Bag End would have made a strong impression on Tolkien. If he did indeed visit in 1923 or thereabouts, he would have found in Bag End a striking contrast to the urban surroundings of Leeds. It was certainly grimmer up north than it is today, especially before the Clean Air Act of 1958, and the city would have existed under a pall of atmospheric

---

[10] Jennifer Paxman. Clock and barograph (affectionately known as Arbuthnot, after the bishop's second name) were given to the Brookes Smiths when Jane moved into her caravan at Blackminster.

pollution, conditions which may have had something to do with the pneumonia he contracted in that year. Tolkien has a notoriously weak chest and his letters are full of references to bouts of illness; living in cities throughout his life in an era where sooty atmospheric pollution was the norm cannot have helped. Whether he was living in Birmingham, Leeds or, later, Oxford, he always hankered after a rural life which existed before industrialisation and suburbanisation. His 1923 trip to Worcestershire must have impressed him with the health-giving qualities of country air. Jane no doubt would have been solicitous, having lost her husband to pneumonia in 1909.

It has to be admitted that the links between J.R.R. Tolkien and Bag End are at best tenuous and it wouldn't do to make too much of them. Documentary evidence is limited. We know that Tolkien visited the place at least once, as he gave a description of its location in the letter quoted above. His first visit may well have coincided with his 1923 journey from Leeds to see his brother Hilary at his farm near Evesham. He must also have visited at one point with his son Christopher, who has vague memories of the place, and it reasonable to assume that this was a family visit in the late 1920s. How Tolkien got there is not known: he bought his first car in 1932, but as Wayne Hammond and Christina Scull point out,[11] England at the time was served by an extensive rail network, including Evesham, and local transport, either by bicycle or taxi made everywhere accessible. Any relevant correspondence between Tolkien and Jane on the subject has disappeared; if Jane had any letters, they were probably thrown out with other paraphernalia when she had one of her periodic clear-outs. Tolkien's published correspondence from this period is also thin on the ground and even if there were any, it would probably be of the mundane sort that would not merit preservation for posterity. Nevertheless, one could go as far as to assume that, particularly with the close proximity of his brother Hilary near Evesham, Bag End and Aunt Jane may have been on his itinerary several times. The house, with its five substantial bedrooms, was certainly of a size to comfortably accommodate the growing Tolkien family. The Brookes-Smith family and Hilary Tolkien's side of the family can clearly be shown to have been visitors to Bag End from the photographic records, but if J.R.R. Tolkien took any snaps they have certainly not seen

---

[11] *The J.R.R. Tolkien Companion and Guide* p.1039.

the light of day. But it has to be admitted that Hilary and the Brookes-Smiths formed more of a social circle around Jane Neave than Ronald, who was at the time preoccupied with a growing family and absorbing professional duties.

Tolkien was well aware of Aunt Jane's ambitious approach to life, and he may have summoned a wry but respectful smile when this most enterprising of his Suffield relatives finally returned to the fabled family roots at Bag End. No other member of that branch of Suffield family had ever achieved so much or aspired to living in such style. It may also have appealed to his sense of fun to see his revered aunt installed as lord of the manor, a position way beyond the dreams of the average Suffield. Old John Suffield may well have seen Bag End as some kind of vindication of his status as old Worcestershire gentry, but J.R.R. Tolkien is unlikely to have harboured any such pretensions. However, the house, the farm and the somewhat isolated rural surrounding cannot fail to have made a vivid impression on him at exactly the time when he was beginning to formulate the places, names and stories that eventually found their way into *The Hobbit*. Typically, he never makes the references explicit, but it is only common sense to imagine that they must be there.

Chapter Four

JANE NEAVE AT DORMSTON

Aunt Jane was certainly an important figure in the early life of J.R.R. Tolkien and his brother Hilary. When Mabel Tolkien and her sons returned to Birmingham and the Suffield household in 1895, Jane was living at home in Ashfield Road and her tall figure and determined personality must have made an immediate impression. The Suffields were a close and affectionate family and the modest size of their house must have meant that they were constantly in close physical proximity. One can speculate with some reason that after the death of their mother in 1904, Jane would have assumed something of a surrogate mother status in the eyes of the Tolkien brothers. At least one can say with some certainty that she kept a maternal interest in both of the brothers for the rest of her life, perhaps with a bias towards the less successful and more vulnerable Hilary. Even though Ronald was ploughing an independent furrow from his late teens onwards, he was nearly always in touch with his aunt, visiting her on several occasions in Nottingham, Scotland and Worcestershire. In the uncertain years of WW1 and its aftermath, it is not unreasonable to speculate that she represented to him some kind of stability in a world that could be troubling and hostile.

Various Tolkien commentators, including myself, have speculated that the physical, mental and spiritual strength of Jane Neave may have made their way into Ronald's fiction. Some people say Gandalf, some Galadriel, some Lobelia, but she certainly had the wisdom and leadership qualities of that old fox of a wizard, and though she was handsome rather than beautiful, the mystical power of Galadriel may also be detectable. For

Lobelia,[1] read her sheer bloody-mindedness. One thing is certain: wherever Jane went she made an impression as a leader and organiser, whether on the Swiss expedition of 1911 that Tolkien alludes to in one of his letters, or the academics of St Andrews University or the agricultural workers of Gedling or Dormston. If Jane had not been the aunt of the famous author, she might not be the figure of interest that she is. On the other hand, her life, which I have documented in more detail in my book *Tolkien's Gedling 1914*, deserves some mention in its own right.

Jane Neave, born Emily Jane Suffield in 1872, was the younger sister of Mabel Tolkien, the writer's mother by a couple of years. Whereas Mabel's strengths lay in the arts and languages, Jane was strongly inclined towards the scientific. It was Jane who taught the young Ronald geometry in preparation for his entrance exam to King Edward's School. From the ages of twenty to thirty three, she taught at the King Edward's Bath Row School in Birmingham, and during this time took a science degree at Birmingham's Mason College, the forerunner of Birmingham University, specialising in botany and physiology. In a letter of 1961, Tolkien refers to this academic achievement, while referring to Jane, somewhat inaccurately, as a "maiden aunt". This is not the only inaccuracy: Tolkien constantly gets her age wrong in his letters, but she was the only other member of his immediate family to hold a university degree and she was, in many ways, his intellectual peer. These scientific interests which bore fruit in a degree, clearly can be directly related to her subsequent farming career. But Jane was also something of an all-rounder: she shared the traditional Suffield interest in literature and had a wide knowledge of poetry, an interest which certainly brought her closer to her nephew Ronald; she was also a fairly competent artist in the charming and somewhat naïve Suffield school, a talent she shared with her father, her sister and J.R.R. Tolkien himself. One delightful watercolour [2] shows a lady – perhaps Jane herself – talking to two little girls as they sit on a farm gate in an idyllic country landscape.

In 1905, she married her long-standing fiancé Edwin Neave, when he was promoted to manager of the Guardian Assurance Company in Nottingham,

---

[1] I am inclined to discount Lobelia, although Tolkien hints she was modelled on an old lady he knew. Jane was not avaricious or unpleasant in any way, although I have no doubt capable of shaking an umbrella in righteous indignation.

[2] A copy of which was given to Maggie Burns by Oliver Suffield. It is a part of the Suffield Family Collection.

and lived in the nearby village of Gedling with Edwin until his death of pneumonia in 1909. Following Edwin's death, she resumed her academic career for two years at Scotland's St Andrews University where she was the warden of University Hall, a women's college. Here she came into contact with Ellen and James Hector Brookes-Smith and between them they decided on a farming venture back in Gedling. This move into farming was certainly a bold one, especially as she had a well-established academic career. At St Andrews she had made a very favourable impression, supervising building, the lay-out of gardens and choosing the furniture and décor of University Hall. The university pleaded with her not to go, but Jane was a determined woman and farming was a career in which a woman could make her mark. There is a striking resemblance here with the decision of Beatrix Potter to adopt a similar career in similar circumstances. Hard work may have been the remedy for a broken heart. Although there are conflicting accounts of her relationship with Edwin Neave, correspondence from later in her life suggest that this move back to Gedling may have been motivated by a desire to return to a place where she had been happy – the place where her husband was buried. In a very much later letter,[3] she asserts she was throwing herself into the kind of hard physical work that took her mind off her recent tragic loss.

A full account of the Gedling Phoenix Farm venture and of J.R.R. Tolkien's connection with that farm, where he embarked on his mythological career with the writing of *The Voyage of Earendel the Evening Star*, can be read in my book *Tolkien's Gedling 1914* along with a more detailed account of Jane Neave's life.

Jane farmed at Phoenix Farm and Manor Farm in Gedling with the Brookes-Smiths between 1912 and 1922. When the farm was sold in 1922, she appears to have lived briefly at Hornets Castle in Devon, apparently a gift from the Brookes Smiths, and this gift may have been part of the settlement arrived at when the Phoenix Farm episode came to an end. Jane did not stay long at this eccentric little house at Sherwell, which still stands today on the edge of Dartmoor. It had been a much-loved country retreat for the Brookes Smith family offering, as Jennifer Paxman observes, "…no facilities whatsoever except the air and the solitude". After this date, Hornets Castle does not figure in Jane's life, so one can only assume she let it or sold it before her return to farming.

---

[3] So far unpublished. I have had sight of this but am not at liberty to reveal the source.

In the absence of relevant correspondence, one can only speculate as to the reasons for the move to Dormston. However, it is not difficult to guess at some reasons. For a start, she was now an experienced farmer, and there is every reason to believe, a successful one. The WW1 period was a busy one for agriculture; Jane would have run a profitable business in Nottingham and probably built up some capital; also, the farm itself was valuable, either as a prime site for supplying the needs of nearby Nottingham, or as potential suburban building land, for which it had been originally earmarked. Her move to a substantially larger farm of over 200 acres might be explained by her successful Gedling venture. In addition to any profits she had from Phoenix and Manor Farms, she had been left a substantial sum in Edwin Neave's will and was also paid by Ellen Brookes Smith for managing the Gedling farms, a sum that was paid in 1922.[4] The evidence is that Jane was a canny businesswoman, but she was also generous, particularly with her nephew Hilary.

In moving to Dormston, Jane was returning to the ancestral county of the Suffield family, just as her nephew Hilary, J.R.R. Tolkien's brother moved to his fruit farm at Blackminster near Evesham in the same year. There is evidence that Jane, who had money, was instrumental in setting Hilary up at Blackminster, for later in life she blamed herself for the hard time Hilary always had in making ends meet in his horticultural career. As it turned out, Jane also probably had difficulties making the Bag End farm pay its way.

Just twenty seven miles south of Birmingham, Dormston was a location much closer to her family and particularly to her widowed father John, then hale and hearty but in his late eighties. It may be that Jane, as the youngest daughter, felt a familial duty to look after John Suffield, and we do know that he spent much time with her at Bag End until his death in 1930. Perhaps her move from Bag End in 1931 was triggered by the fact that she no longer had to look after him.

The rambling Elizabethan look of Bag End would have had an instant appeal to Jane, and her fondness for the farm is reflected in her eventual sales brochure, which is included here as an appendix. From the late Victorian period the well-off had been building for themselves houses in this style, incorporating everything from half-timbered construction (often

---

[4] Information from Jennifer Paxman on Hornets Castle and Jane's management fee from a recently discovered diary entry by James Hector Brookes-Smith.

cosmetic), fancy leaded windows, ceiling beams and vaguely medieval looking doors and door furniture. Among the middle classes of the early twentieth century, there was a strong element of historical nostalgia reflected not only in the revival of traditional English customs – maypoles, folk-dancing and so on – but in architectural styles and such things as Anglo-Saxon names – Edith, Alfred, and Harold. But Jane was buying the real thing when she bought Bag End, and, practical farming considerations apart, she was buying into a little corner of traditional Olde England. Jane had been born a suburban girl and the first thirty three years of her life had been spent in Birmingham. The Ashfield Road house in which she grew up was modest in size and comfortably lower-middle class in nature. Kings Heath was well provided with parks and tree-lined avenues – a pleasant place to be – and dotted around in the more affluent areas, were fake half-timbered building in the manorial style, sporting turrets and overhangs. Even Tolkien's modest childhood home at 5 Gracewell sported mock Elizabethan timbers. But Ashfield Road must always have seemed a kind of suburban exile for the Suffield family, whose family traditions harked back to the countryside of Worcestershire.

In fact, for Jane Neave and old John Suffield, timber frame construction of the Elizabethan period may have held an additional personal association. Old Lamb House,[5] where John Suffield ran his drapery business in the centre of Birmingham in the 1880s was just such a building. John and Jane, who was in her teens when this building was demolished, may well have harboured fond memories of the Suffield shop, destroyed in the name of progress. John was certainly interested in the history of his shop and wrote a history of it.

Now out of living memory, the period of Jane's ownership of Bag End is lost in time. We do know that from 1923 to 1927 she had a partnership with Marjorie Atlee, an ex-King Edward's pupil of Jane's, who had worked on the Gedling farm. The partnership was dissolved in 1927 when Marjorie married Jane's nephew, Frank Suffield at the Dormston church of St Nicholas. (It was with Marjorie and Frank that Jane spent her last years on their small-holding in Gilfachreda near New Quay.) We also know that Jane preferred the older and traditional name of the farm, Bag End, over the alternative Dormston Manor Farm, a choice which shows a

---

[5] I am indebted for this information to Suffield historian Maggie Burns.

measure of good taste and historical awareness over status. Bag End was a farm of considerable proportions, mixed arable and pasture like Phoenix Farm in Gedling, and her venture would have required considerable energy and know-how. As an "incomer", Jane would have had to stamp her authority on the enterprise. Women farmers were not that much of a rarity at the time, but Jane was a particular kind of modern woman with the sort of innovatory ideas that might have raised an eyebrow or two in conservative Dormston. Knowing Jane's determined and independent frame of mind, it is possible to surmise that she would have gained the upper hand in any possible disputes.

In 1931, she sold the farm,[6] but retained two of the cottages, letting one out and keeping the other, Church Cottage, for herself. Two factors may have contributed to her leaving Dormston: one was the death of her father in 1930; the other may have been the severe agricultural depression that hit Worcestershire in the late twenties. However, as she approached the age of sixty, she left Dormston and moved to Chelmsford in Essex to be near the Diocesan retreat run by the celebrated mystic Evelyn Underhill. So, on her retirement from farming she embarked on a determined religious quest which lasted several years and brought her into contact with some of the serious religious thinkers of her day, leading to an enduring interest in medieval mysticism. Born into a firmly non-conformist background (John Suffield was a Unitarian preacher) her religious sensibilities moved gradually towards high Anglicanism, a brand of religion that may have outstripped the plain and modest nature of the Dormston church of St Nicholas. The plaster relief of The Virgin Mary she donated to the church, and which can still be seen on the rear wall, is slightly incongruous in the otherwise undecorated church.

When she sold Bag End in 1931, she retained one of the cottages and in 1937 she returned to Dormston taking up residence in Church Cottage which still stands much renovated and added to, just up the road from the church of St Nicholas. It seems to have been a fairly active retirement, and in the year of her return, she was instrumental in setting up the new village hall and became president of the Kington and Dormston Women's Institute. Jane was a great leader and organiser wherever she went. From this later period, she is still remembered by some of the older inhabitants

---

[6] The details of the sale are given as an appendix at the end of this book.

of Dormston, as an active and respected member of the community, driving her little Ford car, a relative rarity at the time. The funds for the rebuilding of the village hall were dependent on the setting up of some kind of women's club, and who better to give credibility to this than Jane with her strong instincts for the betterment of woman's lot. Not only Jane, but two other previous owners of Bag End, Mrs Milner and the Kemp Homers, were instrumental in the raising of funds and the picture of the opening of the village hall, kindly supplied to me by the current W.I. shows a plethora of local worthies.

Jennifer Paxman, the grand daughter of Ellen Brookes Smith, Jane's partner in the Gedling enterprise, has some vivid memories of Jane in the 1940s at Church Cottage. It was a fairly Spartan two up and two down affair with an outside privy and water from a pump. But its garden with its apple, pear and greengage trees and a frog pond is remembered as something of an idyll by the then teenage Jenny who was versed by Jane in aspects of country lore – where the best mushrooms were available and how to find the "king blackberry". Jane stayed at the cottage for about ten years (she is on the electoral register until 1948). After this we find her living in a caravan on Hilary Tolkien's fruit farm at Blackminster for a few years. Her final years were spent at the idyllic village of Gilfachreda near New Quay in West Wales with her nephew Frank and his wife Marjorie. Although the period of her residence in Dormston is now practically out of living memory, she is still something of a legend in the area in her own right irrespective of her connection with her famous nephew.

Chapter Five

THE NAME BAG END

As I have already suggested, Tolkien himself showed virtually no interest in the name "Bag End". In the whole of his published letters, there is only one reference to the name and that is not even slightly illuminating. One might have assumed that a man who was the president of the English Place Names Society would have something to say on the subject, but perhaps the fact that he didn't tells us simply that it was a convenient linguistic find with phonological link to "Baggins". Yet it has become a permanent feature of his imaginary world, appearing in *The Hobbit* as "Bag-End" and in *The Lord of the Rings* as "Bag End", and as Tolkien people are the kind of people who like to interpret such things, it has occasioned a fair amount of speculation. My own feeling is that when Tolkien chose the name of Jane Neave's farm for his well-appointed hobbit-hole, he was merely making use of a name with which his older children would have been acquainted. Indeed, the three boys had all visited the farm in the 1920s, so it would have been entertaining to find the name used in their father's stories. When Tolkien began *The Hobbit* in 1930, Jane Neave was still in residence, so the humorous reference would have been current. "Baggins" itself, as Tom Shippey has discovered,[1] was a name that Tolkien borrowed from a northern dialect word for a snack, but whether Baggins or "Bag End" first came into Tolkien's consciousness is uncertain.[2] He certainly would have been aware of Bag End from 1923 – quite early in, or even predating, the period of gestation of the hobbit ideas. Whichever came first, the two terms clearly chimed together in a

---

[1] J.R.R. Tolkien, Author of the Century, p.8.
[2] Although Miss Biggins does figure in a story of 1922/23 – *The Dragon's Bay*.

convenient way. The cosily diminutive surname of Baggins is clearly more important in the whole scheme of *The Hobbit* but it is possible that Tolkien's discovery of this word occurred years after his first visit to Bag End. Both "Baggins" and "Bag End" are borrowed from identifiable realities, but it is reasonable to suppose that the name Bag End played a more important part in the gestation of *The Hobbit* than has been generally recognised.

Jane Neave and Tolkien, who was always interested in place names, must surely have discussed the name, as it was Jane's conscious decision to change Dormston Manor Farm back to Bag End.[3] Jane had a habit of changing the names of her farms: in 1912 she had changed the prosaic Church Farm in Gedling to Phoenix Farm. English farm names are often fluid – Phoenix Farm, which had been Church Farm, became known locally as Smith's Farm – all within a period of ten years. Consequently it is not always easy to say what the "proper" name of a farm is; it is, effectively what people call it. In the case of Bag End, though, we do know that Jane didn't make it up: when she bought the farm in 1923, she found that the farm she had bought as Dormston Manor Farm was called Bag End in the deeds, and decided to revert to the original. It was a decision that Tolkien would have approved of, the preference for the no-nonsense old English name over the French "Dormston Manor" with its Norman associations. From Domesday till the eighteenth century, the manor of Dormston had been passed from one aristocratic or at least well-heeled family to another, but the name Bag End somehow suggests the essentially earthy Englishness of the place. It is also the name that appears on Ordnance Survey maps as "Bagend". At least it is quite possible that Jane's conscious decision to revert to the English name might have focussed Tolkien's attention on its toponymic implications.

Various commentators [4] have picked up on the similarity between the name Bag End and the French *cul-de-sac* and the subject is one that commonly arises in Internet discussions. It is almost certainly the case that Tolkien noted the similarity and found it amusing to give Bilbo and Frodo's comfortable home a name which happens to be a direct translation of the

---

[3] This information from Jennifer Paxman. It is an important fact with obvious implications for Tolkien's fiction.

[4] I would recommend Tom Shippey's entertaining treatment of the subject in *J.R.R. Tolkien, Author of the Century*. Here he argues that Bag End is the name of the road rather than the dwelling. He may be right up to a point, but it's hard to see how a road can have a doorknocker.

name that often appears on suburban road signs. In doing so he might have found some pleasure in taking a side-swipe at the pretentious French term. After all, we are dealing here with the literary associations of the name, and, in his very careful nomenclature, Tolkien certainly had something of the kind in mind.

In reality, however, the origin of the name Bag End has nothing to do with *cul de sac*. On one level it is just a matter of dates: according to the O.E.D., the term cul de sac in its present meaning only comes into currency after 1800; the French term is anatomical, referring to a part of the intestine, not to roads at all. Indeed the French do not use this term and how it came into its present use is obscure – possibly some kind of joke. We know that the name Bag End existed before 1800, so unless we accept the unlikely premise of some witty peasants translating a French medical term, we must conclude that it is not a translation.

On the other hand, there is some evidence that Bag End may have been more of a "dead end" in the early 18th century before the main aspect of the house was changed from north to south facing. As I have surmised in a previous chapter, and as Jane Neave guesses in her sales brochure, the Elizabethan house probably faced north towards what was the village of Dormston. Nowadays Dormston consists of a few scattered farms and cottages, as it did in Jane Neave's day, but it is possible that there was a relatively late desertion of the village to the east of the church. In this case, access to the manor house would have been from the north as opposed to the later western access from the north-south lane which now leads to Dormston from the main road.

Bag End is not a "nickname" as some have suggested, as it was well established over the centuries. "Local name" makes more sense but what else are all names but local? Perhaps here the implication is that "Dormston Manor Farm" is the non-local name – the official name – and there may be some sense in this. It is true that people local to Dormston insist that Bag End is the proper name for the place, and perhaps in this they are cocking a snook at upper class pretentions, aware that through most of its history Bag End was either the residence of wealthy incomers or absentee landlords. It is certainly the English name, as opposed to the Norman one. However, it is just conceivable that there may be a reference to the

5. The Name Bag End

topography of the farm: on a map, we can see that the farm itself and its home fields could be seen as a sort of point between the lane and the Winterbourne [5] stream on the east. This feature is noticeable from a map or an aerial photograph but to what extent it would have presented a striking resemblance to the end of a bag from the ground is doubtful. On the other hand, it is true that Bag End stood at the eastern boundary of Dormston from ancient times. In this case, Bag End would be a description of the general area, and "farm" would tie it down to the specific building. The idea that Bag End originally described an area rather than a building is supported by a conveyance deed of 1733 which mentions "the close or ground in Dormstone commonly known as Bag End."

If this simple topological reference is not the origin of the name, we need to look further back in time. In her sales brochure of 1931(see appendix) the two 15th century dovecotes are said to constitute "an interesting link to the Manor of Dormstone, by which title the property was originally designated". This suggests that Dormston Manor was indeed the older name, but this theory depends on how far back you are prepared to go, and perhaps you have to go back before the Norman Conquest to find the original.

"Manor" is a Norman administrative term, but when Dormston is listed for taxation purposes in *The Domesday Book*, the compilers merely adapted the details of an existing Anglo-Saxon settlement dating back before the time of King Edgar, when it is described in a charter. Attached to one of the five "manses" mentioned in this charter may have been Bag End in a previous incarnation. So although the current house dates back to 1582 and the dovecotes to a century and a half before, it is quite possible that there was some substantial structure on the site in Anglo-Saxon times. If so, it must have had a name, and where better to start than Bag End?

The *bag* root is a common one in place names of Old English origin. One possibility is that it is a personal name: if we look through Anglo-Saxon names, we find a variety of possibilities – Baecga, Bacga, Baega, Bagga, Baga for example.[6] In this case, Bag End would signify something like "the

---

[5] "Winterbourne", a common English name for a stream that only flows in the winter, is marked on the sales brochure map and is also mentioned in the medieval boundary limits of Dormston. It must have been this stream that supplied the two ponds at Bag End. The stream still appears on contemporary maps although it may have been piped underground for practical reasons.

[6] These so-called "monothematic names", consisting of one element, were typically peasant names or nicknames. Only the ones ending in a double G were pronounced as in *bag*. Baecga, for example would have been pronounced as in the modern badger.

boundary (ende) of Bægga's land". In favour of this derivation is that Bag End does indeed stand at the eastern boundary of the manor of Dormston. However, Eilart Ekwall in his English Place Names, points out that the bag root is never combined with settlement names like *ham* or *tun*, rather with words for physical features: there are no Baghams, and no Bagtons, although there are Bagleys (*leah* being a clearing) and a Bagshot (shot = Old English *sceat* meaning a strip of land). He points out that in other Germanic languages *bag* can denote certain animals, sheep in Scandinavia, pigs in Holland (Old Dutch *bagge*), for example, and that in English the word may be a "significant word" rather than a personal name. He also points to the name Bawdrip – *drip* meaning trap, and although he can only guess at the meaning of the *bag* root, he thinks it could signify a fox or badger. In this case, Bag End would be an area associated with those animals. *Bag* might be an unrecorded dialect name for an animal of some kind but probably not a badger: there is a perfectly good Old English word for badger, *brocc*, a Celtic borrowing, and the word badger is only recorded from the fifteenth century. Consequently, the word badger has probably nothing to do with it. In Old English, this would have been *brocc* and in fifteenth century English, it would surely have been simply Badger's End. As I suggest above, there is a possibility that Bag here is simply what it means today, as it could be argued that there is a certain topological bag-like nature in the location of the farm between the lane and the stream. But if the name is indeed a really old name, there are no other really old English place names incorporating *sack* or *bag* in this sense of the word. It is worth noting, however, Tolkien's invention of "Sackville" as in the Sackville Bagginses, is certainly playing on sack as a synonym of bag, although the satire is in the pretentious *ville* element, *sacc* being a perfectly good Old English word, more common, in fact that the Norse *bag*.

The *end* element is problematic when suggesting that Bag End is an Anglo Saxon place name. It is, in fact a rare occurrence in place names of that era, and where it does appear, it tends to be in a mutated, almost unrecognizable form as in *In*gate or Detch*ant*. So although Bag End may well be of Anglo Saxon origin, denoting either the boundary of Baecga's land or a place where animals of that name are found, it would be a rare occurrence. Places like Mile End and Southend are of later dates than the

Anglo Saxon period. In general the use of the *end* element in major place names such as in the London suburb of Ponder's End, which dates from exactly the same date as the Elizabethan rebuilding of Bag End, denotes the boundary of Ponder's land; Wallsend denotes the end of Hadrian's wall; Lane End in Flintshire tells us where the lane ends.

The *bag* element remains mysterious but apart from the specific signification of *end* mentioned above, it is likely that something vaguer may be denoted: today, we sometimes use the word end in the loose sense of a general location or area as in "the other end of town" and there is some evidence of this colloquial usage in a document of the 17th century where two churchwardens style themselves as "'John Morris of the buttystile and John Morris of the upper end'.[7] In this case, *end* would seem to denote a general area of local significance and across England there are numerous examples of this usage which date from medieval or later times. So the *end* element may suggest a homely, almost affectionate name for a well-known local area or dwelling. In this sense, it does indeed fit with the idea of a "local" name. It was an element sometimes adopted in 20th century fiction to suggest something of the rural past, as in E.M. Forster's *Howard's End* or Mole End in *The Wind in the Willows* (a favourite book of Tolkien's). This nostalgic connotation would certainly have had an appeal for Tolkien suggesting, as it does, somewhere off the beaten track – a place of repose and seclusion.

If this is the case, the *end* element may be of post Elizabethan origin: it was certainly there in 1731, where the farm is recorded on an estate plan [8] as "Bag Inn". Bag End is an extremely unlikely location for an inn, being well off the main road, but there is still a remote possibility that Bag End was for a time known as Bag Inn. It is an intriguing idea, and although one is inclined to dismiss it as a clerical error at a time in which spelling, especially provincial spelling, was approximate, the rest of this estate map of the parish seems to have been produced with meticulous attention to detail. Is it just possible that in the period immediately following the end of the Russell dynasty's ownership, the building found another temporary use or was simply renamed before being improved again in the late eighteenth or early nineteenth century? Possibly during early 18th century period Bag End

---

[7] Churchwardens' Presentments from The Vale Of Evesham, 1660–1717: P. Braby – *Vale of Evesham Historical Society Research Papers,* 1975, V, pages 61–69.
[8] WCRO Ref: BA 1101.

might have fallen into a state of disrepair in the hands of a yeoman farmer who found this massive old house too much to cope with. Arguing strongly against this possibility is Robert Savage's conveyancing document [9] of 1733, which gives the first reliably recorded mention of the name as "Bag End".

In the end, place name research is dogged by vagueness and controversy with different authorities giving entirely different etymologies for Anglo Saxon place names. There is much that is down to speculation and I suppose I have merely added to it. Having started out with some definite ideas, I have to admit that all I have achieved is to lay before you certain possibilities. In the final analysis such speculation lies well beyond the boundaries of any Tolkien interest. There is no evidence that Tolkien attached any significance to the *origin* of this unusual place name, although eventually a significant cluster of ideas formed around the name which have resonance in *The Hobbit* and *The Lord of the Rings*. As to the speculation about *cul de sac*, one can confidently say that this is not the origin of the name, although this does not invalidate the kind of attention Tolkien scholars have lavished on the term from time to time. Their ideas make entertaining reading and it is probable that Tolkien did have some such intention when he chose the name for the dwelling of the Messrs Baggins. It is homely, humorous and unpretentious – just the kind of thing he was looking for.

---

[9] WCRO Ref: 2219.

APPENDIX

The following document, reproduced with permission of the Worcestershire County Records Office, (Ref: 2919) was prepared in May 1931 prior to the sale by auction of Bag End at The Grand Hotel in Birmingham. It is interesting not only because it gives a detailed account of Bag End at the time, but also a little of its history. Jane Neave herself seems to have had a significant input into the document, which reveals the pride she took in Bag End as well as her detailed interest in the farm.

BY DIRECTION OF THE OWNER.

Worcestershire.
Parish of Dormston, near Inkberrow.

8 miles from Alcester; 11 miles from Worcester and 27 miles from Birmingham.

Sale by Auction of

THE EXTREMELY INTERESTING FREEHOLD

Residential & Agricultural Property

KNOWN AS

BAG END

comprising the very beautiful red brick and half-timbered Historic

Residence of the Tudor Period

of great antiquarian interest, having panelling and other interior oak in its original state.

TWO VERY RARE XV CENTURY DOVECOTES

constitute an interesting link with the Manor of Dormstone, by which title the property was originally designated.

The Accommodation includes:

OUTER & INNER HALLS, THREE RECEPTION ROOMS, SIX BED & DRESSING ROOMS & BATHROOM, GOOD WATER SUPPLY AND DRAINAGE SYSTEM, together with the extensive MODERNISED FARM BUILDINGS,

the whole forming an artistic group in the Elizabethan manner, lying in

201 ACRES

of sound land with frontage to a good road; also

Two Useful Cottages and Gardens

in good order. VACANT POSSESSION OF THE WHOLE (except one cottage) ON COMPLETION.

CHESSHIRE, GIBSON & CO., F.A.I.

---

will offer the above for Sale by Auction (as Lot A), at

The Grand Hotel, Colmore Row, Birmingham,

On THURSDAY, 21st MAY, 1931,

at Four o'clock in the afternoon.

FURTHER PARTICULARS of—

The Solicitors: Messrs. MUSGROVE, LEE & ARTHUR SMITH, 18, Newhall Street, Birmingham.

The Auctioneers, at their Offices, COLMORE HOUSE, 21, WATERLOO

General Remarks.

SITUATION.

BAG END is situated in the Parish of Dormston, approached by excellent roads, and being 2½ miles from the village of Inkberrow, 8 miles from Alcester, 11 miles from Worcester, and 27 miles from Birmingham.

THE SITE

is probably that of a much older house, since the present house itself has Manorial Associations probably arising out of the original manor, dating from Edward the Confessor. In the Conqueror's reign, William, son of Corbucion, held Dormston of the Abbot of Westminster.

THE FARM BUILDINGS.

These are well placed for easy administration and have been equipped with modern improvements at considerable expense.

THE LAND

is sound and the proportion under the plough is small.

HUNTING

with the Worcestershire and Croome packs.

SHOOTING.

The shooting on the property is in hand.

WATER SUPPLY.

An adequate supply of water for all purposes is obtained from a well in Yard, pumped to Storage Tank, with soft water auxiliary supply.

DRAINAGE to cesspool in O.S. 40.

POSSESSION.

Vacant Possession of the whole of the Property will be given upon completion, with the exception of the one Cottage and Green's Orchard. Possession of these may be obtained as indicated in the Sale particulars.

Stipulations.

THE PLAN.

The Plan is for reference only. The Vendor does not bind herself as to its accuracy. No error thereon shall annul the Sale.

THE CULTIVATIONS.

The descriptions of the cultivations of the various Fields, as set out in the annexed schedule, are believed to be correct, but no claim shall arise on account of incorrect description.

TENURE.

The Property is Freehold. There is a Tithe, payable to Queen Anne's Bounty, amounting to £2 1s. 8d. per annum, and a Land Tax of 13s. 2d. per annum.

TIMBER.

The growing Timber, belonging to the Vendor, is included in the Sale.

FIXTURES.

All such Fixtures as are usually designated " Landlord's Fixtures " are included in the Sale. No Tenant's Fixtures are so included.

TENANCIES, TENANT'S CLAIMS AND TENANT RIGHT.

The Property is sold subject to the Cottage Agreement, the nature of which is described in the Particulars of Sale. In the case of the Lands of which Vacant Possession is given to the Purchaser, the Vendor shall be treated as an Out-going Tenant and the Purchaser shall be treated as an In-coming Tenant, and shall, therefore, pay to the Vendor all such sums as are properly payable presuming this relationship to be existent. The Vendor shall not, however, be responsible for any claim for dilapidation or deterioration.

EASEMENTS, ETC.

The Property is sold subject to all rights-of-way (whether public or private), water, drainage, electric, telephone or other easements, quasi easements and privileges that may affect the same, and a Purchaser is deemed to have notice of same, whether they be mentioned in these Particulars or any abstracted documents or not. Further, the Purchaser shall take over the Vendor's rights and liabilities (if any) in the occupation or other roads.

RESERVATION.

The Vendor reserves the right to hold a Sale or Sales by auction on any part of the Property, at any time prior to the date fixed for completion of the purchase.

𝔥istorical 𝔑otes.

In the description of a property possessing, apart from its agricultural and residential value, so great an antiquarian and historical interest as does Bag End, it is felt that no excuse is necessary for dealing at a little more length than the usual with this latter aspect of the property.

The Parish of Dormston is described by Nash as a curacy in the upper division of Pershore Hundred, and in the Deanery of Pershore. Originally, the Parish either formed, or was part of, the Manor of Dormston, which, in the Conqueror's reign was included in the lands of St. Peter of Westminster.

As to whether the present house stands upon the site of the original one is uncertain, but what is certain is that in Bag End, known previously as Dormston Manor, we have a perfect example of a late sixteenth century manor house. It is probable that the residence was largely re-built about the time of a Sale or Lease of the property in 1582, by John Russell (whose family had held the Manor for several centuries) to Richard Buller and Richard Cholmeley.

"Say—is there beauty yet to find?
And certainty? and quiet kind?"

The existence of a manor house upon the site much prior to 1582 is evidenced in one of the Dovecotes, the lead-work of which bears the date 1413, this date being a quarter of a century after the family of Russell succeeded to the Manor, following de Valence, Earl of Pembroke.

The present house is largely late sixteenth century, although parts would appear to date back to the period of the building of the Dovecote referred to.

The original building, which was half timbered, was probably " L "-shaped, and faced upon a forecourt on the North side. A later addition to the South elevation probably occasioned what appears to be a change of front, since the principal entrance is now on the South side, overlooking the garden.

A feature of the interior of the house is the delicately designed Tudor panelling, in splendid preservation and of considerable value.

Allied with this also are a perfect example of a Tudor staircase and several very fine fireplaces and carved surrounds of the same period.

Some of the panelling and doors seem to date to a much earlier period than that suggested as the origin of the present house.

To the antiquarian, perhaps, the chief interest in the property will be the Dovecotes, which have already been mentioned in passing.

A splendid studded door on the east side. The door on the south side was of a similar plank construction, but disappointingly neither door was circular. These massive doors may well date back to a time when Bag End was a semi-fortified manor house. The early years of the house span an era of lawlessness and feuding and John Russell's application for a "license to crenellate" in 1388 suggests something of an earlier lawless Worcestershire countryside.

Jenny and Julian Brookes-Smith in 1930 receive a pipe-smoking lesson from their father, Colin. The Brookes-Smiths were regular visitors at Bag End and the two girls visited Jane at Church Cottage in the 1940s. The photographs of Bag End in this book were mainly taken by Colin Brookes Smith, a close friend of Jane Neave over a period of fifty years. It is thanks to his photographs and memoirs that I have been able to piece together previously unknown aspects of Jane Neave's life.

XI

The house seen from the orchard pool to the west of the house. The main entrance to Bag End was to the right of this.

This view of the workshops from the main entrance, a slightly enhanced version of an image in Jane's sales brochure, shows some of the neat and well cared for grounds of Bag End. The building on the right is the gabled dovecote, by this time "put to more practical use".

XII

A playful heifer and a camera-shy bull ("Valencia Ambassador") Bag End was primarily a cattle farm, with only about a quarter of the land devoted to arable. Jane delighted in her livestock here and previously at Gedling.

XIII

The colourful relief of the Virgin and Child that Jane donated to St Nicholas' Church. It is the only splash of colour in the charming but otherwise undecorated church. After her sojourn with the Christian mystics in Chelmsford, Jane seems to have embraced a quasi-Catholic form of religion which can be seen in this icon. Her musical tastes took a similarly mystical direction with her devotion to the wonderful music of Hildegard of Bingen. Julian Brookes Smith was also named, perhaps at Jane's behest, after Julian of Norwich, another woman mystic.

The 1937 opening of the village hall. Jane returned to Dormston in 1936/7 and became a founder member and president of the W.I. She also made some financial contribution to the building of the hall, as did two other previous owners of Bag End. Jane, pillar of the community, can be seen fourth from the right in the background wearing a hat.

Worcestershire meets Birmingham. Tolkien painted a similar view of Kings Norton church. This view is from Wast Hills. Now high-rise Birmingham looms in the background, but much of the area Tolkien explored in his childhood and teens is still relatively unspoilt, four miles from the city centre.

A view of the Malvern Hills from the British Camp. Clearly visible from Bag End, The Malverns were a destination for Tolkien and C.S. Lewis on walking tours.

XV

The porch of the church of St Nicholas Dormston, a couple of hundred yards from Bag End. Jane was a worshipper here and maybe this picturesque doorway featured in the future imagination of Tolkien.

XVI

Colin Brookes Smith's snapshot of the church of St Nicholas. The porch and tower predate Bag End by a century.

A monumental brass image of John Russell, Richard II's Master of the King's Horse and the first Russell to own Bag End.

The Dovecotes.

These are noted in a book on the subject by Mr. A. O. Cooke, as follows:—" Two Dovecotes stand in the garden of Bag End Farm, Dormstone, each holding between 500 and 600 nests. One, slightly the smaller of the two, has a four-gabled roof and

*"The moan of doves in immemorial elms,
The murmur of innumerable bees."*

four windows, and bears the date 1413 upon some lead-work." From the same source, " It is to be understood that for many centuries the right to erect and maintain one of these structures was strictly limited. Those so favoured in the Norman laws were the Lords of Manors, which included not only a vast number of land-owning laymen, but also abbots and other ecclesiastics, the parson of a parish being frequently among the number."

Particulars
of
BAG END
DORMSTON.

THE RESIDENCE, built of red brick and gabled on South front is half timbered in North, West and East elevations. It is built in the manner of the 16th Century with a layout which is probably Elizabethan.

THE APPROACH to the house is by an imposing entrance and drive from a good road within ¼ mile of a first class main road. In the foreground is an ornamental garden with lawns and flower beds, encircled by a number of stately elms.

The Land

is well lying and attractively placed.

ACCOMMODATION:

Charming panelled entrance lobby.

Panelled Inner Hall

(17ft. by 15ft.) with stone-flagged floor and delightful open fireplace.

Leading off are—

Study

(12ft. by 8ft.)

9

Lounge

(17ft. by 13ft. 6in.) with extremely attractive open fireplace with Dutch tiles, carved oak ornamental surround in period with the Tudor panelling.

Store Place

Back Hall

(North front) with flagged floor, beamed walls and ceiling and original stone recess, forming a portion of the original Chapel. Herefrom is principal staircase.

Bathroom

with bath, lavatory basin (H. & C.) separate W.C.

Inner Hall

(East wing) with flagged floor and store cupboard and having secondary staircase to first floor.

Leading off are—

Dining Room

(17ft. by 15ft.) with part flagged floor and Dutch tiled hearth, beamed walls and ceiling.

Large and cool Dairy

Off side passage—

Kitchen

with range, sink and boiler.

Store

adjoining, containing an "Ideal" boiler, supplying constant hot water and also heating radiator in bathroom.

At the rear of the main hall is the principal staircase to first floor. It is a VERY FINE STAIRCASE with balustrading in original condition as carved in Tudor times. Under these stairs screened by a fascinating carved and panelled oak door with original iron lock and hinges is a WINE STORE.

ON THE FIRST FLOOR.

Main Landing

No. 1 BEDROOM (17ft. by 16ft.)—adjoining are LADY'S POWDERING ROOM & GENTLEMEN'S DRESSING ROOM, each room having its original elm floors.

No. 2 BEDROOM (16ft. 6in. by 14ft.) with oak panelled walls and carved and tiled fireplace surround.

No. 3 BEDROOM (19ft. 6in. by 18ft.) having original elm floor, beamed ceiling and a magnificent fireplace of Tudor design with massive carved oak surround and panelling.

Off side Landing

(and approached also by secondary staircase) are two bedrooms (16ft. by 14ft. 6in.) and (16ft. 6in. by 14ft.) each having dormer window and beamed ceiling.

On the second floor—

Storage Room

𝔗𝔥𝔢 𝔊𝔞𝔯𝔡𝔢𝔫𝔰 𝔞𝔫𝔡 𝔇𝔬𝔪𝔢𝔰𝔱𝔦𝔠 𝔒𝔲𝔱𝔟𝔲𝔦𝔩𝔡𝔦𝔫𝔤𝔰

include flower gardens with lawns and productive kitchen garden with fruit trees and two orchards. A delightful feature of the gardens are the two half-timbered Dovecotes of antiquarian interest and picturesque appearance. These links with the manorial associations of the property are now used for more practical purposes. The one having been converted to use as a VERY ADEQUATE GARAGE and the other as a GARDEN HOUSE AND POTTING SHED. On the North side are a covered carrying way and an enclosed Fold yard with WATER STORAGE HOUSE.

" *Where tangled foliage shrouds the crying bird*
And the remote winds sigh—and waters flow."

The Farm Buildings

are conveniently grouped on the North and East side of the house, they include:

1st FOLD YARD.

Cow house with Calf pen adjoining.

Mixing house and Granary.

2nd FOLD YARD.

Well equipped modern 14 tie Cow house with Head range and covered carrying way.

Mixing house and Calf pen adjoining.

Large five bay Barn.

OPEN FEEDING YARD with brick Shed and Calf pen having concrete floor.

Bull pen.

Three modern Pig styes.

IN RICK YARD—Two useful Implement sheds and Cart hovel.

THE STABLING which is a picturesque half timbered building includes—Four Stalls, Loose box, and Harness room with Loft over (see photograph).

NOTE.—The live stock quarters are of a high standard, they have only recently been modernised, including new drainage system, and there is a water storage tank in Fold Yard No. 2.

13

The Cottages

There are two Cottages included in the Sale. The one is situated in O.S. 11 and comprises a brick built four-roomed Cottage and Garden with pump water, let to Mr. H. Blizzard, at the rent of £13 per annum (tenant paying rates) upon tenancy requiring six months' notice of termination expiring Lady Day or Michaelmas. To the same tenant is let the adjoining Pleck, being O.S. 10 and known as "Green's Orchard" at a rental of £5 per annum. The second Cottage O.S. 31 known as "Church Cottage" situated near St. Nicholas' Church, is a four-roomed brick Cottage with Garden, at present let upon a tenancy expiring on the 24th June, 1931, when vacant possession may be obtained.

THE PROPERTY is in the occupation of Mrs. Neave who will give possession of the whole with the exception of the one Cottage and Orchard referred to.

The Schedule

No. on Sale Plan	DESCRIPTION	CULTIVATION	QUANTITY A. R. P.
39	House, Buildings, Yards, Garden		2 0 9
43	Pond	Water	20
38	House Orchard	Pasture Orchard	3 0 15
40	House Field	Pasture	16 2 4
43a	Walk Orchard	Pasture Orchard	2 18
43b	Perry Mill Orchard	Pasture Orchard	3 23
41	The Bank	Arable	6 3 22
42	Wheat Leasow	Arable	8 2 14
42a	Wheat Leasow	Arable	1 29
77	First Berrow Field	Arable	10 0 23
78	Middle and Far Berrow Field	Arable	17 0 26
44	Rowan's Orchard	Pasture	6 1 24
46	Lower Leys	Pasture	9 1 23
35	Church Meadow	Pasture	18 2 36
1048	Wood Ground	Pasture	24 3 4
14	Wood Field with Shed	Pasture	11 1 1
13	Long Ground with Shed	Pasture	9 0 1
12	Foss Ground	Pasture	11 2 18
10	Green's Orchard with Cattle shed	Pasture Orchard	3 39
9	Green's Wood	Wood	17 2 4
5	Green Hill (with Shed)	Pasture	20 3 33
11	Cottage and Garden		1 14
31	Cottage and Garden		37
4	Little Green Hill	Pasture	4 0 34
			201 3 31

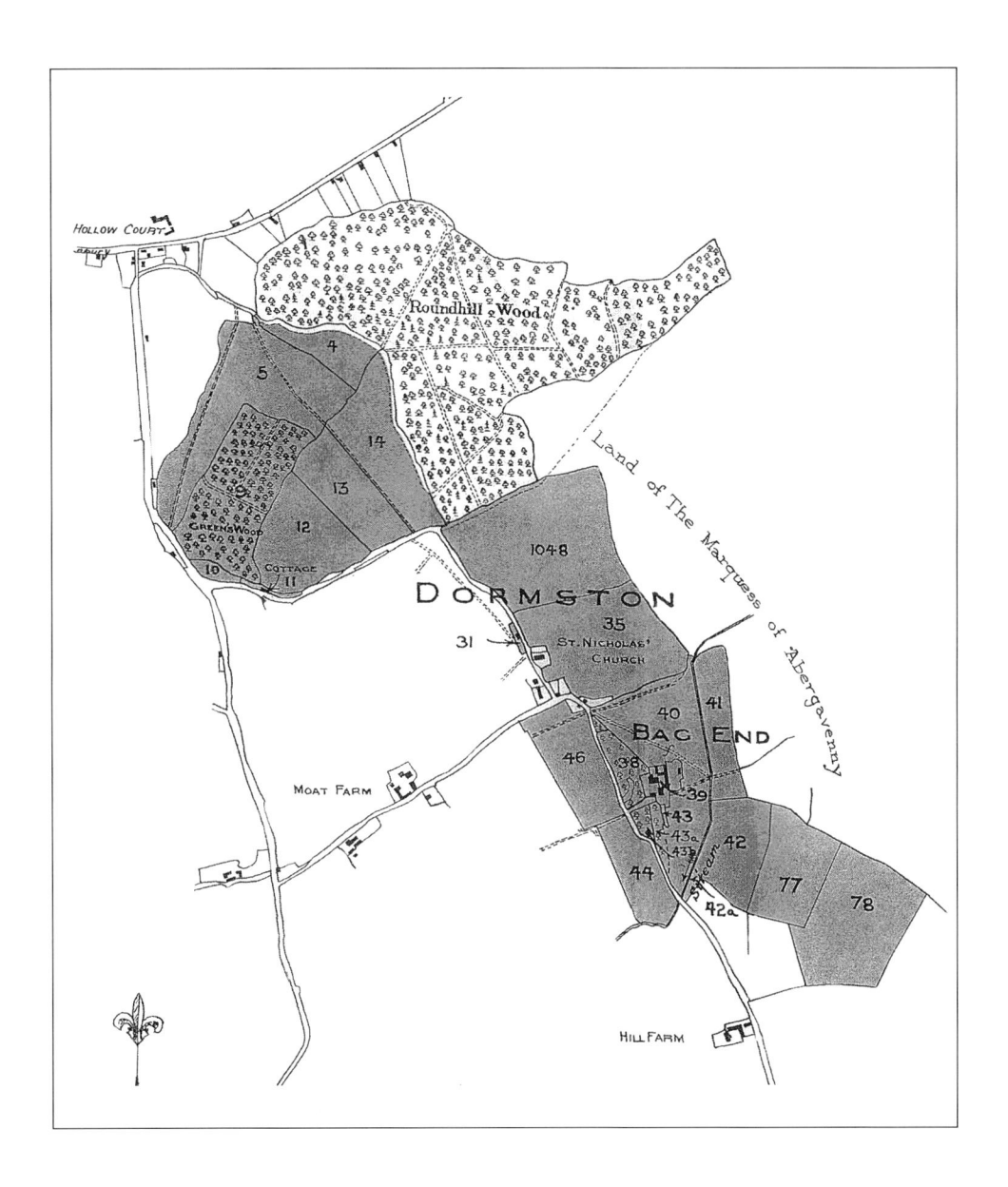

Appendix

RECOMMENDED READING

Books referred to
Tolkien's Gedling 1914 – Andrew Morton and John Hayes.
J.R.R. Tolkien Artist and Illustrator – Wayne Hammond and Christina Scull – Harper Collins.
J.R.R. Tolkien, Author of the Century – Tom Shippey – Harper Collins.
The Lord of the Rings – J.R.R. Tolkien – Allen and Unwin.
The Hobbit – J.R.R. Tolkien – Unwin Books.
The Concise Oxford Dictionary of English Place Names – Eilart Ekwall.
The Letters of J.R.R. Tolkien – Ed Humphrey Carpenter and Christopher Tolkien – Harper Collins.
J.R.R. Tolkien: A Biography – Humphrey Carpenter – Allen and Unwin.
Mr Baggins – John D. Rateliff – Harper Collins.

E-Texts
The Place – Names of England and Wales – Rev. James B. Johnston, M.A., B.D. (Internet Text).
A History of the County of Worcestershire Vol.4 – William Page, J.W. Willis-Bund (editors).
Worcestershire Anglo-Saxon Charter Bounds by Della Hooke, P.

Archives
The Worcestershire County Records Office.

Photographs
All photographs with permission of Jennifer Paxman.

Except
Dormston Bag End Staircase – WCRO Photographic Survey Ref: 9101.
Pictures of over mantels at Bag End – WCRO Ref: 6716, 6718.
Dormston – Bag End Manor, Pigeon house barn and outbuildings Ref: 9096.
Dormston – Bag End Manor Studded door Ref: 9908.
The picture of John Russell by permission of the Monumental Brass Society.
The picture of the opening of Dormston Village Hall by permission of the Kington and Dormston Women's Institute.
Photographs of The Malvern Hills. Kings Norton from Bilberry Hill, the church door at Dormston and Jane Neave's presentation plaque by the author.

INDEX

Archers, The 2
Atlee, Marjorie 15, 31

Bag End
   the manor house, vii, Ch. 2,
   throughout
   the name 8, Ch. 5, throughout
   the building 11, 12, 13, also
   appendix and illustrations
   farm 14, 15 also appendix and
   illustrations
   fictional Bag End Ch. 3,
   throughout
   possible Tolkien visits viii, ix, 24, 25
Baggins(es) vii, viii, 22, 23, 34, 35
Bengworth 3
Blackminster 6
Brookes-Smith(s) ix
   Colin 1
   Ellen 29, 30
   James Hector 29
   Julian X
Buller, Richard 9

Cholmeley, Richard 9
Clent Hills 1
Cul de sac theory 35, 36

Dormston, throughout
   Name 8
   St Nicholas' Church ix, 32
   enclosure 11, 14
   late desertion of 8
Droitwich 1

Elgar, Edward 7
Eomer 20
Evesham 2

Feckenham Forest 12

Galadriel 27
Gandalf 27
Gedling 29
Gurney, Ivor 7

Harvington Hall 12
Holst, Gustav 7
Hornets Castle 29
Howells, Herbert 7
Hwicce, the people 4

Inkberrow viii

Kemp Homer 33
Kidderminster 2,
King Edward's School 3, 23, 31
Kings Heath 1
Kings Norton 1
Kington and Dormston W.I. 32

Ladywood 1
Lewis, C.S. 5
Lickey Hills 1
Lobelia Sackville-Baggins 27

Malvern Hills 5
Mason College 3
May Hill 7
Mercia, Mercian dialect, 4, 20
Milner 33
Moat Farm ix, 9, 11, 24
Moseley 1

Neave Edwin 28, 29
Neave, Jane throughout
   academic career 28
   at Phoenix Farm 29
   at Bag End and Dormston 30–33

Old Lamb House 31
Paxman, Jennifer vii, 24 (footnote) 29, 33
Peter Jackson 19
Phoenix Farm 29, 32, 35

Rateliff, John D. 22
Richard II 8, 9
Russell, John, (1551–1593) builder of Bag End 9, 10
Russell John, (1310–1349) Master of the King's Horse 8

Sarehole 1, 19, 22
Savage, Robert 40
Saxton map 9
Sayer, George 5
Shippey, Tom 20
Shire, The 7, 19, 20, 21
Speed map 9
Strensham 8
Suffield, family ix, 2, 3
Suffield, Frank 15, 31
Suffield, Oliver 28 (footnote)
Suffield, John 3, 6

The Hobbit throughout
The Lord of the Rings throughout
Théoden 20
Thomas, Edward 7
Tolkien Mabel 3, 28
Tolkien, Christopher 4
Tolkien, Hilary ix, 6, 27, 30
Tolkien, J.R.R. throughout
   Bag End as source for fiction 20–26
   references to maps and illustrations 20–23
   relationship with Jane Neave 26, 27, 28
   Tolkien's Gedling 1914 vii, 29

Vaughan Williams, Ralph 7

Worcestershire – Ch. 1, throughout

ABOUT THE BOOKS

My two biographical sketches, *Tolkien's Gedling 1914* and *Tolkien's Bag End*, are concerned with the author in a landscape. In each case it is the kind of unremarkable, homely English landscape that underscores most of our lives in one way or another, just as the woods and fields of Phoenix Farm were, unknown to me at the time, one of my childhood playgrounds. For the author of fiction, such places provide a rich stock of memories that can be summoned up in future years.

Yet while part of his imagination soared in the realms of fantasy, there was a part of this very homely and domestic man which always looked back to the golden age of his childhood at Sarehole, where he and his brother roamed the fields and woods and exercised their imaginations with fairytale inventions. It was vision born in the morning of the world, when everything was fresh and the adventure of life had just begun. Dark years lay ahead for the young Tolkien – the death of his mother and The First World War – but it was during these years that he began to work on his mythology of Middle Earth, an era that began with the remarkable Earendel poem the first draft of which was written at Phoenix Farm. In his two great works of fiction, *The Hobbit* and *The Lord of the Rings,* The Shire, a version of ordinary English folk in ordinary English places, has a central role as the starting place and end of both adventures. Hobbiton, with its farms, its mill, its gardens and quiet domesticity, is a composite not only of Sarehole, but of places like Dormston and Gedling too. If home is where the heart lies, Tolkien's heart lay in exactly this kind of quiet English landscape.

ALSO AVAILABLE

Tolkien's Gedling 1914, Andrew H. Morton and John Hayes,
ISBN: 978-1-85858-423-2, published by Brewin Books, priced £9.95.

In late September 1914, J.R.R. Tolkien, his life in crisis, visited his Aunt Jane's Phoenix Farm in Gedling near Nottingham. The poem he wrote there on September 24th, *The Voyage of Eärendel the Evening Star*, was the spark that ignited the whole of his later mythology.

Focussing on this single event, Andrew Morton and John Hayes set out to discover more about Phoenix Farm, Jane Neave and the poem. *Tolkien's Gedling*, which contains over thirty previously unpublished photographs, explores the social changes in Gedling that gave birth to the Phoenix Farm project. It also contains much original material for the Tolkien enthusiast, including the fullest account so far of his influential Aunt Jane, whom many have taken to be the model for his famous wizard, Gandalf.

1